THE SOUTH

Edited By Tessa Mouat

Years of

First published in Great Britain in 2016 by:

YoungWriters

Coltsfoot Drive
Peterborough
PE2 9BF
Telephone: 01733 890066
Website: www.youngwriters.co.uk

SB ISBN 978-1-78624-490-1
Printed and bound in the UK by BookPrintingUK
Website: www.bookprintinguk.com
YB0286A

FOREWORD

Welcome Reader!

Have you ever wondered what it would be like if you stepped back in time? Well, for Young Writers' latest comp we asked our writers nationwide to travel back in time and create a story of up to 100 words with a beginning, middle and end – a hard task indeed!

I am delighted to present to you 'Ancient Adventures - The South', a collection of ingenious storytelling that covers a whole host of different topics. Just like me you will be transported to all types of different adventures and, I'm sure, will learn something new with each story you read. From vicious Vikings to escaping evacuees, this book features it all and provides the most exciting, thrill-provoking escapades with every turn of the page.

The standard of entries, as always, was extremely high so I'd like to congratulate all the talented writers featured in this collection and, as you step back in time, I hope you find as much enjoyment reading these mini sagas as I did.

Tessa Mouat

CONTENTS

Amber Miller (10) 56
Alex Lind (10) 57
Lara Poulsom (10) 58
Libby Bullen (10) 59

Ditcham Park School, Petersfield

Brogan Meehan (10) 60
Jack Keeping (10) 61
Jemima Butler (10) 62
Annie Rowley (10) 63
Daniela Dobby (10) 64
Will Goldmann (10) 65
Jake Last (10) 66
Hattie Cobden (10) 67
Jake Jones (10) 68
Miles Barber (10) 69
Freddie Lock (10) 70
Winston Smith (10) 71
Joseph Handley (9) 72
Amelia Taee (9) 73
Hatty Wood (10) 74
Qetsiah Joachim-Baggott (9) 75
Finn Lewis (9) 76
Oliver Osgood (9) 77
Harry Soden-Bridger (10) 78
Matthew Saunders (10) 79
Cecily Brown (9) 80
Tom Duddridge (10) 81
Theo Cable (10) 82
Sebastian Hopkins (10) 83
George Henderson (10) 84
Francesca Walmsley (10) 85

Downs Junior School, Brighton

Maizy Day (10) 86

Dragon School, Oxford

Dana Aben (10) 87
Alexander Phelps (9) 88

Farringtons Junior School, Chislehurst

Ciara O'Neill (10) 89
Maria Manta (11) 90
Nicki Kardel 91

Georgeham CE Primary School, Braunton

Flo Benfield (10) 92

Great Tew Primary School, Chipping Norton

Isabella Blundell (10) 93
Hattie Souch (11) 94
Sophie Wilson-Fry (10) 95
Finlay Beggin (11) 96
Jamie Levene (11) 97
Blythe Ferguson (10) 98
Reuben Anthony (9) 99
Matilda Mackie (10) 100
Gethin Collins (11) 101
Victoria Louro (11) 102
Archie Leigh-Wood (10) 103
Scarlet Floyd (11) 104
Eliza Carleton Paget (11) 105
Amber Owen (9) 106
Jennifer Tambini-Aylett (11) 107
Archie Grant (9) 108

Oasis Academy Long Cross, Bristol

Roy Quartey (11) 109
Imogen Davies (10) 110
Michael Court (11) 111

Nayeema Akther (11) 112
Kieran Cotterill (11) 113
Mason Pike (11) 114
Isabelle Stinchcombe (10) 115
Holly McCarthy (11) 116
Isabelle Howie (11) 117
Natalia Gnatowicz (11) 118
Regan O'Connor (11) 119
Courteney Mazur (11) 120
Joanna Milkiewicz (11) 121
Fynnlay Booker (11) 122
Stanley Scrivin (11) 123
Louise Thomas (11) 124
Jade Checketts (10) 125
Harrison Bishop (11) 126

Pitton CE Primary School, Salisbury

Mya Dinning (10) 127
Amy Puryer (11) 128
Theo Evans (10) 129
Ruaridh Thomson Easter (10) 130
Imogen Ryan (9) 131
Finn Bergstrom (10) 132
Evelyn Lush (11) 133
Josh Key (10) 134
Oliver Chalke (11) 135
Perran Akib (10) 136
Finn Sainsbury (10) 137
Alexandar Kadiev (9) 138
Daisy Acreman (11) 139
Ella Azzopardi (10) 140
Sophie Buxton (11) 141
Sean Parker (11) 142
Jess Mossman-Smith (11) 143
William Horsfall (10) 144
Faith Hellyer (11) 145
Ruby Mann (11) 146
Tomas Bozic (10) 147

Ramsgate Holy Trinity CE (A) Primary School, Broadstairs

Charles Westby (10) 148
Noah Shakeshaft (10) 149
Louis Benedict-Evans (10) 150
Georgiana Michael 151
Jack Welsh (9) 152
Lucas Harris (10) 153
Jennifer Allan (9) 154
Ella Goldwin (10) 155
Betsy Bridger (10) 156
Timothy Allan (9) 157

Seend Primary School, Melksham

Freddie Hubert (11) 158

Southcott Lower School, Leighton Buzzard

David Kryklyvyy (8) 159

St Andrew's CE Primary School, Sherborne

Olivia Bowditch (10) 160
Reuben Crocker (9) 161
Izzy Ward (9) 162

Whitehorse Manor Junior School, Thornton Heath

Makeda Powell (9) 163
Tamar March (9) 164
Ijeoma Nwaonu-Aghaluke (9) 165
Godfrey Nkansah (9) 166
Hodan Ereg (9) 167
Christian Andrews (9) 168
Omar Qamar (9) 169
Lucas Victorire-Carter (9) 170
Aleena Nadesan (8) 171

Cachelle Sullivan (9)	172
Emmanuel Serwornu (9)	173
Luca Tanase (9)	174
Naima Maxwell (9)	175
Caylin Spruit (9)	176
Richard Sava (9)	177
Ewura Akua Asare (9)	178
Fiona Krasniqi (9)	179
Samuel Ponou (9)	180

Whitleigh Community Primary School, Plymouth

Grace Glattback (8)	181
Ryan Ryder (8)	182

THE MINI SAGAS

Scramble!

'Scramble!' shouted the captain.

I loaded my plane with enough bullets then jumped in. Ferociously, I zoomed up the runway. The sad sound of guns flew through my innocent ears. The Nazis got there before us. We always fought over Hertford. *Bang! Bang! Bang!* Planes crashed and the birds scattered from the trees! Blood and guts were everywhere. Suddenly, *bang!* I woke up in a hospital bed.

'Where are all my friends?' I asked the nurse.

'Don't worry, Private Henry, they're all fine,' she spoke softly.

I peeled the sheets off of my body to reveal...

Lilac Montanaro (11)
Bayford CE Primary School, Hertford

The Chase!

Seriously, the tour guide was so annoying! Then I found a secret passenger in the middle of the pyramid. It was so cool. Right behind me was a mummy! I was face-to-face with a real mummy! Running quickly, the mummy chased me through the scorching-hot desert. Exhausted, I sat down on the tall, strong rock.

'Hi,' a boy chirped.

'Hi,' I replied. Then I saw him take apart the exact mummy that was chasing me through Egypt. He told me it was a mummy with a remote control and it was his own toy mummy!

Tigerlilly Pike (10)
Bayford CE Primary School, Hertford

The Roman's Fight

'Quick, we don't want to lose this battle, do we?' said the emperor, giving us our shields and swords. Suddenly, I found myself rushing towards the enemies. With one push of a mighty sword, the emperor was dead! 'Nooo!' I screamed, as my head fell to the ground.

As the sun settled and we won the battle, the floor was nothing but bodies and blood. The next morning was our payment day. I was so excited, my first one! I wondered how much I would get. 'Salt! I've got salt!' Unbelievable!

Frankie Hardey (10)
Bayford CE Primary School, Hertford

The Arrow Of Hastings

Blood flew through the smoky air as William sliced off the frowning head of one of Harold's knights. Harold, William's mortal enemy, was beginning to come into sight. Light bounced off William's sword, half-blinding one of the opposition's knights. It lead to a kill. Eventually, Harold and William were face-to-face, no knights between them. Meanwhile, one of William's archers, Canconcordo, known as Arrow Guy, was scanning the battlefield for his king. When he found him battling Harold, he only had one thing on his mind. An arrow hit - not the king, Harold's horse. It flattened the king, he died.

Will Crone (10)
Bayford CE Primary School, Hertford

ANCIENT ADVENTURES - THE SOUTH

The Chase

Creeping silently, Rosa and I wandered through the emerald jungle, as the trees swayed and the birds danced through the sky. *Roar!* Then we heard it. 'What was that?' Rosa bellowed, clutching her fists by her side. Suddenly, a daring dinosaur thrashed towards us. What should we do? Were we going to die? Would we be safe? My jaw dropped; I felt like I couldn't move until Rose held my hand. Then we ran for our lives until her hand left mine and I couldn't see her running next to me. 'Rosa!' I yelled. But she wasn't there. She'd gone.

Jessica Chappell (11)
Bayford CE Primary School, Hertford

Cut-Throat Callam And Knitting

Black smoke poured out of the dilapidated chimneys of the Viking huts. Cut-Throat Callum was out hunting for a deer when he stumbled across a shivering lamb. If you think that Cut-Throat Callum was a vicious Viking, well, you thought wrong! He was a big softy when it came to baby animals. When Cut-Throat Callum came back from a successful hunt, he couldn't help taking the lamb with him. While Callum was eating his dinner, he wondered what it would be like to knit. The next thing you know, jumpers were everywhere.

Maddie Hardey (10)
Bayford CE Primary School, Hertford

The Mummy's Trail

One holiday, a few children travelled to Egypt on a pyramid holiday and they saw the tomb of Tutankhamun. They told each other scary stories of Tutankhamun. They all went further into the tomb and bats flew all around, in all directions. They found a key and there was an old crooked door with bandages all over it. They were all up for going into the tomb further and so they did. The room was pitch-black and there was an open coffin and a tall black figure slowly walked up to them. They ran for their lives!

George Ward (10)
Bayford CE Primary School, Hertford

Death Island!

Leaves fell from the tree as I sat reading on Death Island, where no one ever came back alive. The wind blew as I heard a mysterious noise going past me. My heart felt like it was about to explode as it came closer. I leapt down from my tree and followed the noise, in and out of the bushes. Then out of nowhere came a big, scaly, ferocious animal. I was face-to-face with a dinosaur. Its mouth widened and a terrible grin appeared. My jaw dropped and I went to scream but nothing came out. *Crunch!*

Isabella O'Reilly (10)
Bayford CE Primary School, Hertford

Julius Caesar Is The Worst

One hot day, I was fanning Julius Caesar. He was sweating and he had a great big, shining ruby. It helped him run the city and one day he forced me to clean it so he could see his face in it so I rubbed and scrubbed and then I ran out of the palace and into a pub. I asked them to hide it. Julius Caesar marched towards me so I rushed out of the pub and the manager gave me the ruby. Then I rushed to the palace and I made a deal with Julius.

Kieran Walden (11)
Bayford CE Primary School, Hertford

Mark The Soldier

Once there was a boy called Mark. He was not long born. He had just gone to sleep when a bomb hit the hospital.

Twenty years later, his mum came to see him. She nearly dropped dead in happiness that he was alive. She woke up Mark.

'Son, can you hear me?'

'Yes, Mum,' Mark said.

Gloomy darkness filled his mum's face.

'What's wrong, Mum?' Mark asked.

'You've got to go to war!'

Mark marched into war. It seemed like miles but he finally made it to the trench. It began...

Ethan Webb (10)
Burbage Primary School, Marlborough

Me And My Dinosaur

I sat up, brushed off the dust and there, sitting before me, was... a dinosaur! I backed off, then its big, long, dribbly tongue licked my face. I was covered in dino dribble. Suddenly, it picked me up and gave me a hug.
'What's your name?' he said.
'Bella', I replied. 'You can speak!'
I have been living with him for seventy years now and still he hasn't changed a bit.

Olivia Weremijenko (10)
Burbage Primary School, Marlborough

What's Life Like As A Tudor Wife?

Splash! The first victim is beheaded, first Katherine of Aragon divorced and now Anne Boleyn beheaded. Pure blood, nice and fresh, splashes everywhere from Henry VIII's special gold and black dagger. 'Ha, ha, ha time to celebrate with pies, delicious chicken and gravy pie, ha, and maybe after I'll have a cherry pie. Yum,' exclaimed Henry. Henry was now desperate for a new wife. Jane Seymour was perfect. They got married in Henry's garden on a beautiful day. She loved Henry and still did even when she died two weeks after giving birth to Henry's only son.
'No!' shouted Henry.

Renee Hawkins (10)
Burbage Primary School, Marlborough

Death Is Awaiting You!

I scream. It is coming, the speeding silver bullet, coming straight for my quick-beating heart. All I can do now is wait. Wait for the two forces to collide. Any moment now, 3, 2, 1... it hits.
I open my weary eyes. What is this place? As I begin to take in my new surroundings, I notice some peculiar people. Who I think are cavemen to 'Vile Victorians' and even 'Rotten Romans'. No one seems to be talking. Wait, is that Winston Churchill? Oh look, there's Blackbeard the pirate! Suddenly, everyone screeches, 'Welcome to Hell!' Then I start screaming...

Olivia Barnes (10)
Burbage Primary School, Marlborough

I Wish I Hadn't!

I stepped inside the small, dusty room. Stumbling over the floorboards, I scrambled across the floor towards a corner. There, in front of me, stood an old, ancient coffin. I stepped back and headed for the exit. Spinning round frantically on the spot, a creak echoed round the room. The door of the coffin opened and a pair of great beady eyes looked down at me!

Spinning round on the spot, I raced towards the door then turned my head. I stopped. Nothing there apart from the empty coffin. I spun round without thinking, that was a mistake... Oh no!

Imogen Rowland (10)
Burbage Primary School, Marlborough

To The Moon And Back - Maybe?

Jack was sitting in his room, bored, on his phone. His friend had just cancelled the play date. He saw on Instagram a picture: 'What have you always wanted to do?'
'I've always wanted to travel to space!' Then he had an idea. He made a potion that sent you up. Fart potion! He put it in his mouth and he zoomed straight away into the sky. A few minutes later, he was surprised to see Neil Armstrong floating in space! Then he landed on the moon. 'Arr!' He took a breath. Little did he know it was his last.

Polly Hobden (10)
Burbage Primary School, Marlborough

The Pyramid

'Hurry up everyone, I'm waiting for this pyramid to be done by next week - you mustn't let me down!' I was getting very impatient. They had been working on this project for two weeks and I'd given them four weeks. They hadn't even got halfway. I was worried that the pyramid might not be done in time and that the gods wouldn't be impressed with me. I just needed to relax.

Suddenly I heard a loud growling noise. I was petrified. Then I saw 'it'. A tall, fearless, dribbling monster. It was my time...

Amy Carey (10)
Burbage Primary School, Marlborough

Waiting For Morning

They were coming. The village was drowning in screams of children watching their lives being ruined. They took all we had, they didn't care. I rushed to my hut, took my possessions. I had no choice now but to run. I ran as far as my legs would carry me. After a good twenty minutes I was done. I had nothing left, nothing but one thing. Courage. I picked myself up again and started a walk that eventually turned into a run. I ran to the nearest den and waited, waited until I woke from this nightmare, waited for morning...

Lisa Nordlund (10)
Burbage Primary School, Marlborough

The Smilodon

I pulled back my bow and launched my death stick. It hit the smilodon like a truck. It stuck in the animal and soon its chest was covered in black sticky blood. It cried out for a time then it fell. It was the alpha, the pack was still hunting for blood.
Four days later, my tribe was arriving at the ceremony and my chief spoke. 'We are gathered here today to...' Suddenly, the air was filled with the growls of a smilodon. I managed to pull out my dagger, it came towards me. I lunged at it...

Luke James-Yates (10)
Burbage Primary School, Marlborough

Pure Blood

All eyes were on me. Vigorously, I gulped. A cold drip of blood, fresh blood, fell on my neck. It was a matter of time before the slim, metal bird swooped down on my neck... With one chance left, I kicked the malevolent executioner aside and wriggled out. Avoiding the cold-hearted security, I hitched up my skirt and ran. I had no time to look at the furious mob behind me. I kept running; only for my precious life. I slipped on some mud. Desperately I tried to get up. The aggravated crowd, with eyes flickering, closed on their target...

Leonie Onis (11)
Burbage Primary School, Marlborough

Opening Night

7.50pm. The players were waiting for kick-off time. Lallana passed to Alli, he whipped the ball in, Kane couldn't get to it. After fifteen minutes there were few chances. But Alli got the ball in again, Kane went for the volley but he missed the ball. In the second half, England created more chances. It was getting late in the game, Harry Kane had the ball but he was tackled by a Russian defender. It was a free kick. Alli took it... top right corner! It was stoppage time and Russia equalised. Final score was one all.

Jai Smith-Little (11)
Burbage Primary School, Marlborough

Boudicca

Boudicca was fighting at an old farm, people lay dead with swords in their chests and daggers in their arms. A couple of years later, Boudicca's husband Prasutagus died. Boudicca kept on fighting on the farm day after day, even more dead people were lying side by side, swords clashing together. One day, it was beginning to look more like Boudicca would get killed by the Romans. She finally decided to die without getting stabbed, so she found a bottle of poison and drank it up. She died later that night in her sleep.

Scarlett Ruta (10)
Burbage Primary School, Marlborough

Untitled

I'm waiting for the battle to commence. I was finally let out again. Let out to a sandy arena. All the two-legged creatures had some sort of hard thing on their chest and their head, and they had a stick with a sharp pointy thing on. Next, another creature threw his pointy stick. I dropped down and the pointy stick missed and speared another creature. Another two-legged creature swung a long sharp object at me but I jumped to the right. The two-legged creature let go of the long object. It was now just me and him...

Harley Britten (11)
Burbage Primary School, Marlborough

The Big Game

This was it. Time for kick-off - England vs Russia. Dele Alli whipped a cross in but it was too hard for Hurricane. Again, a ball went into the box, it was missed again. England went back into the changing room happy with their performances but still no goals. Russia came out and put in a good shift but Russia's defender brought down Kane on the edge of the box and Dier scored. Russia's wide man whipped a ball in and their danger man did a looping header - it was in! They had equalised in the last minute!

Jack Cady (10)
Burbage Primary School, Marlborough

Sabertooth Horror

My teeth were gritted. My sweaty hand grasping the smiloden cub I'd killed earlier. I could almost feel its breath on me. It was close. I held my breath. It pounced, its claws digging into my flesh. This was it, unless... I reached for my dagger, grabbed hold of it and dug it into the creature's fur. It staggered away, yelping in pain. I seized the opportunity to escape. The animal burst out from the trees, my bloody dagger still in it. I ran like my life depended on it. It did.

Ruby Johnson (9)
Burbage Primary School, Marlborough

The Interrogation

When I came in, I was shocked; the weapons room was absolutely bare! All of the weapons in Asgard had been stolen! I stormed into the living room where Thor was having a cup of ale.

'All of the weapons have gone, all of them!'

Thor's jaw dropped. 'Bu-but... my hammer!' he stammered.

'Yes', I said, my voice full of worry. 'Me, mighty Odin, stolen from! If we're going to invade England we must have an interrogation!'

Every person in Asgard was searched and they finally found out Frey, a peaceful god, had stolen the weapons to stop the invasion.

Rory Scott (9)
Clifton College Prep School, Bristol

The Blur-Like Battle

When my friends and I jumped into our longship, I looked back at the village, as if I was never going to see it again. I turned around, seeing the glittering sea, facing the battle ahead.

'You're only 16, Knut Rountrisson. Are you ready?' asked Bjørn.

'Yes,' I replied. Now I saw a monastery, waiting for attack. Our boat hit the bank. 'Go!' I yelled.

We piled out and ran up the beach. It was all a blur. I heard shouts, screams and my sword slashing. Eventually the blur stopped. We victoriously returned to the welcoming village with the treasure.

Rhys Rountree (10)
Clifton College Prep School, Bristol

My First Raid

I could not see land, but I knew it was there. All of a
sudden, I saw it; monks fleeing from a monastery,
just as Knut had said. I jumped out of the boat and
ran towards the monastery, the wet grass on my
legs. Then I saw a monk and changed direction. I
could see him now and I was catching him up.
Thud! I had fallen over a rock and my head was in
some hollow.
'Get up, Gunnar!' shouted Knut. 'The monk has
gone now.'
'My family won't be happy,' I said.
'Curse Loki!'

Toby Denner (10)
Clifton College Prep School, Bristol

Odin's Activity

I was walking around in Essex when I saw a figure and it looked like an old man with a black eyepatch. Tall, two birds, scary. He came again and again and I heard, 'Hello!' I ran and ran and then I heard, 'Alfred.'
'Why my name?' I said.
Then I saw him fully, very tall and he chased me until I came to a tree and then the figure said, 'I am Odin and I need you!'
He took me to a dark and mysterious place and there it was - the Sword of Dreams. Wow!

George Millett (10)
Clifton College Prep School, Bristol

The Gold Crucifix Raid

I remember the attack very well, still to this day.
When we left Scandinavia, we asked the chief what
it would be like.
He replied, 'I'm not completely sure.'
The next thing I remember is scrambling off the
boat and a figure saying to me, 'You are Trygve,
the trustworthy one.' That was when the attack
started, with us leaving the boat and approaching
the monastery. When we got there, some of us
went for jewels, while others went for the slaves. I
became famous as the Viking warrior who brought
back the gold crucifix of Lindisfarne.

Emily Murray (10)
Clifton College Prep School, Bristol

Raid At The Monastery

I, Eirik Giuggiolison, had just sailed across the North Sea. I could see a monastery and a group of monks with their weapons ready for battle. Our chief, Bjorn, shouted, 'Attack!'

We all evacuated the longship with our weapons held in our hands. Before long, I found myself running back to our ship, carrying a load of booty. Behind me was Bjorn with some slaves he was going to bring on board. I looked back and saw the monastery we had destroyed. Eventually, I was back on board steering the ship to Sweden. It was a happy feeling.

Giacomo Giuggioli (10)
Clifton College Prep School, Bristol

The Raid Of Ulf Ghoshisson!

I was sailing in the North Sea. It wasn't going well, the breeze was going in the wrong direction so it was hard for us. Suddenly, there was a strong gust of wind that launched us in the right direction. Someone yelled, 'I can see land, Master Ulf Ghoshisson!'

I saw a monastery and was so happy. We jumped out of the longship and charged at the monastery. I was filled with joy. I smelt beer and bread, it was fantastic. We grabbed as much booty as we could and then set the monastery alight. They'd never forget our visit!

Tanaya Ghosh (9)
Clifton College Prep School, Bristol

The Viking Warriors Raid Britain

My Viking friends and I sailed across the North Sea and left Scandinavia behind us. I was very nervous when land came into sight. I jumped off the ship with my bow, arrows and trusted dagger.
We raided the monastery, tearing it apart. People were shouting, 'Ulf! Ulf!' I remember running back to the ship, carrying all the loot. The booty was extremely heavy. I don't know how I managed. We were finally setting sail again. I went back to my loving family, but I knew I would have another battle to fight all too soon.

Nina Nissim (10)
Clifton College Prep School, Bristol

Untitled

We were travelling fast up a river in my longship. I was rowing when one of my friends shouted, 'Monastery ahead!'
We all got out of the ship except the people with bows and arrows. I took my sword and stabbed a monk in the chest. Another monk with a stick was running at me, so I banged him in the nose with my shield. I dispatched him with my dagger and ran inside the monastery. I remember seeing a lot of gold everywhere. I took all I could carry and then I heard a voice say, 'Torstein, we're going!'

Gaspar Valentin (10)
Clifton College Prep School, Bristol

Getting Treasure

Rolf and his warriors were ready to invade, swinging their swords and running towards the monastery. They saw people carrying shiny treasures. They crept up, hiding around corners. There were people crowding someone and Rolf wondered who it was. If everyone was so amazed at this person they could steal the treasure with no trouble! They found the gold, tiptoed to the boat. Suddenly, somebody shouted, they had been seen! They all jumped into their boat. The king's guards followed. The king was the person that had been crowded. The warriors rowed quickly, but didn't know where to. Nobody knew!

Cassandra Moran (10)
Clifton College Prep School, Bristol

Valdemar And The Mysterious Ship

Finally, on the land where the scared monks hid, hoping in desperation, stood Valdemar the vicious Viking. He slaughtered anything in sight. Suddenly, he caught one and pulled him by his stringy hair, and slung him straight into an enormous tree! Valdemar stormed off like an elephant and kicked the door of the treasure room violently open! He found a monk there, took his axe and split the poor man's innocent skull. He loaded his sack with lots of luxurious jewellery and gold. Then, just as he turned to leave with his sack of shining gold, the ship was gone!

Andy Small (10)
Clifton College Prep School, Bristol

The Missing Boat

The Vikings got ready to fight and were about to set sail. That second, they realised that their boat was missing! Five Vikings went to get another boat and a while later, the Vikings were back. They set sail. They sailed over to a little island off the coast of Scandinavia because they thought that someone there may have stolen the boat. They were very mischievous and always in trouble. Later, they arrived at the little island but they didn't see anything apart from dead bodies and their boat. No one would ever know what happened to the other Vikings.

Hattie Rochford (9)
Clifton College Prep School, Bristol

My 50th Raid

I was on my 50th raid, this was very important for me. I got my axe, 'Bone Breaker', my shield, 'Body Basher', and put on my helmet. Our plan was to get on shore as quickly as possible and take everything. Then somebody shouted, 'I see land, Rolf Faustingson!' Next we went ashore. I destroyed everything in sight, apart from the valuables. I was surprised by how easy it was to raid a monastery. So much treasure and literally no defence! This was easy, especially for someone of my experience. I would tell these tales for evermore.

Taiki Faustino (10)
Clifton College Prep School, Bristol

The Beast Fight

Once, in AD 900, a very friendly farmer called Erik went to cut his corn. The sky suddenly went dark, it became cold. Standing there was a huge creature. This enormous beast was hairy and as black as the midnight sky. He whispered in a deep voice, 'You are my dinner!' When he came near, Erik used his whole strength, took his scythe and stormed towards the monster. Erik fought and fought but the monster wouldn't give up. After a while, the beast looked scared. Erik turned and saw his dog scaring the monster away. No one saw it again.

Julius Baumbach (10)
Clifton College Prep School, Bristol

The Brothers

Spears were flying, they started to attack. People roared as we rowed closer. Once we reached the shore, the fighting started. Warriors dropped all around, blood coloured the water. We attacked, slowly people dropped. I felt guilty after watching people die. I ran to the church, took the gold, ran out, got to the boat and hid it. I, Victor, was looking for my brother who had been stolen. I looked in all the houses except for one. I ran in and shouted, 'Erik?' He was sleeping, covered in blood. I picked him up, ran to the boat and rowed.

Thomas Kipling (10)
Clifton College Prep School, Bristol

My Viking Saga

I was out in the middle of the North Sea, there was a breeze carrying us towards Britain. Despite this assistance, it was taking days to reach Britain. Supplies were low, but everyone was still confident. Suddenly, someone shouted, 'Land!' We rushed to the side of the boat and got ready to attack. I put on my helmet and gripped my sword tightly. I pushed my way to the front and jumped out onto the shore. Rushing towards the monastery, slaughtering monks, I grabbed some gold and silver. The journey home to Scandinavia would be a happy one.

Charlotte Warren (10)
Clifton College Prep School, Bristol

The Monster In The Sea

Everything was quiet and still. Ulf and Snorre only heard the sea. Suddenly, all was dark and a loud growling noise startled them. They turned and saw the monster, its hungry eyes staring at them. Its eight legs ready to grab them both. Ulf threw his axe at the monster. Snorre did the same, but nothing worked. The monster looked at the axe and smiled. Then Snorre realised that he had forgotten about his spear. He grabbed it and threw it at the monster's heart. The monster looked at him, fell back into the water and was never seen again.

Johanna Baumbach (10)
Clifton College Prep School, Bristol

Dojo And The Chariot

This is the story of Fiery, a king cobra from Egypt. He was brought to ancient Rome. This is where our story begins. Fiery was captured by General Nestor and brought to Rome. There he met the comedian, Dojo, who was a desert monitor, but they became friends. Fiery's job was to fight, but his plan was to escape. Dojo dug a hole, he got out. Fiery got stuck at first. Dojo climbed into a moving chariot and bit the driver. The chariot crashed, destroying the cages. All the animals escaped so Fiery and Dojo sailed on towards ancient Egypt.

Theo Laredo (10)
Clifton College Prep School, Bristol

Raiders Of Britain

Torestien thought his son, Rolf, would be a great raider, but Rolf didn't agree, he hated raiding! Rolf's dad had made him lead a crew at thirteen years old. Not to mention that this was on a longship with people he didn't even know! Rolf was scared of these shady characters, but luckily there was one person he knew. Ulf was his best friend and had been since they had arrived in Britain. The raid went well and as quick as lightning, they got all the loot! Rolf happily smiled as he journeyed back home to tell his proud father.

Jonathan Morley-Cooper (10)
Clifton College Prep School, Bristol

The King Of Sea Raids Britain

We started our journey across the North Sea to Britain in our trustworthy longship. After a few days on the North Sea, we could see land. When we reached the land, we jumped out of our boat 'The King of Sea' and ran to start the raids. Inside the monastery, there was gold everywhere, jewels wherever you looked and the monks weren't even putting up a fight. I grabbed all the treasure I could carry, a few slaves, and then got out of there. As soon as we all got to the longship, we sailed back to Norway, joyfully singing.

Megan Cook (10)
Clifton College Prep School, Bristol

A Raid On Lindisfarne

I was only 16 when I went on my first raid of a British monastery. I remember the man in charge of the boat yelling at me, 'Sigurd Morrison, stop the boat!' We all scrambled out of our longship, advanced menacingly on Lindisfarne and grabbed everything we could. The monks pleaded, but we had no mercy. Eventually, I stood there with several barrels of beer, a chest full of gold and a monk at my feet. We sailed back to Norway with triumphant grins on our faces, singing and joking happily together with treasure at our feet.

Poppy Mumford (9)
Clifton College Prep School, Bristol

The Pack

The huge hammer was pounding down hard on the wood. It was dark, Arne was holding the torch while I chiselled away at the wood. We were building a boat by the gloomy forest. I kept hearing unsettling noises in the woods. They were getting louder and louder. I could hear a pack of wolves howling, then suddenly, one pounced on Arne and started ripping him, limb from limb. I ran up to the hungry wolf, its vicious eyes staring at me. I thought I was going to die. Quickly, I punched it, knocking it out and killing it instantly.

Oscar Wright (10)
Clifton College Prep School, Bristol

The Longship

It was a bright, sunny day. Olav walked in and started building the longship with Ulf and Magnus. He looked out of the door and he saw something strange. He looked around the corner and there was a strange man standing. He ran off. He came back and told his story of how he liked to stand and watch the boat building. His name was Rolf. Once they finished the longship, it was time for battle. The warriors were back with lots of treasure and gold. Soon enough, it was time for another battle. They left, never returning.

Olivia Warfield (9)
Clifton College Prep School, Bristol

The Fast Starvation

The rain was tipping it down, the crops were withering, my people were dying. We had no choice but to invade the Saxons. Lots of my warriors were dying of starvation and so was I. I couldn't go unarmed! I only had five warriors. We finally arrived at midnight, they were mostly all asleep, we went to the closest farm. Suddenly, they heard us going back to the boat before we could get another load. A battle began, we fought bravely, only losing one warrior. With a famous victory under our belts we returned, victorious.

Imogen Isaacs (10)
Clifton College Prep School, Bristol

The Midnight Raid

It was midnight in Norway and I had been rounding up men for a raid. Just as we got on the boat, 'The Arne Youngingsson' - named after me - I gave the command to pull away. We crossed the North Sea to a land called Britain. The light wind carried us swiftly to our destination. And then, suddenly, we saw glorious Britain and a monastery! Finally it was time for the raid. I charged out with my men behind me, my sword swinging rapidly. In the monastery I grabbed every gold item I could find and plenty more besides.

Jude Young (9)
Clifton College Prep School, Bristol

Bibles, Gold And Slaves

It all started when I, Trygve Forestisson, embarked on my first Viking raid. I climbed aboard the longship and sat down. I was now an oarsman. Days later, a storm broke out and my arms ached. Luckily, it cleared and we rowed up onto land. We saw a large monastery. We clambered out and raced inside, swords held high. I collected Bibles, gold and importantly, slaves. I felt pride as I did so. We were now in Britain, I raced back to the boat with my booty and started rowing back to cold Scandinavia. I felt incredible.

Poppy Forestier Walker (9)
Clifton College Prep School, Bristol

The Voyage

I stared at the sea. I, Magnus Erikson, son of Erik Olafson, chieftain of my village, had to prove myself by attempting a treacherous quest. I had to sail out in the world to find and explore foreign lands. People said I was brave, in truth I was terrified! The sea was a dangerous and frightening place. I had only ten men and one longship, a gift from my father. When I thought about it, all my family's honour was in my immature hands. The captain of my longship arrived. He was ready to sail out to sea. Was I?

Simon Hormiere-Marquie (10)
Clifton College Prep School, Bristol

The Deadly Day

It was AD 797 and I was waiting in my castle, afraid that something would happen - it did. I heard a loud roar! And it was there, a loud, gigantic monster. I started running, the wind was howling, the pebbles tumbled and I accidentally dropped my sword. I picked it up and ran quickly while the monster chased me. I kept running but then I turned around and the monster wasn't there so I kept quiet and tried to hide behind a bush. The monster was there so I took my sword and cut his head off swiftly.

Gianluca Cosci (10)
Clifton College Prep School, Bristol

The Raid

I, Ulf Scottison, was setting off with my crew over the North Sea, preparing to raid England. I had my dagger in my hand, ready for battle, and I was commanding my people where to go. Finally, I could see England, it was a few miles in front of us. When we got there, we stopped our longship and got into position. We had started the raid. Monks ran indoors, our crew was unstoppable. We were kicking doors open, slashing at the monks, and soon they were all gone! We got our booty and set off back towards Norway.

Soloman Scott (10)
Clifton College Prep School, Bristol

Poor Old Ulf

'Timber!' The first tall tree fell and Knut got the axe and started making the boat. 'Timber!' Another tree fell, but this time was followed by a cry for help, Leif came running. Out of the wood a tree fell on Ulf! However, Knut was no help, he just fainted - Leif thought long and hard. Eventually, he got it! He was going to use Knut's axe to cut the tree in half and roll the end part of the tree off Ulf, then take him to the medicine man. When Leif went to look, the tree was gone!

Ben Byas (10)
Clifton College Prep School, Bristol

Ragnar The Raider Hairy Breeches

As my clan and I were sailing through the ocean, I wondered if I, Ragnar Hairy Breeches, would survive this raid but I dismissed the thought. I was the best raider ever! As we reached the shore, I saw Ivar the Boneless and his men awaiting us on the beach. We cried a war cry and we started. As I fought like the Beast of Red Mountain, I looked to each side and realised all my clan were dead and I was surrounded. Ivar the Boneless disarmed me while I wasn't looking and threw me into a pit of snakes!

Otis Cervera Hernandez (10)
Clifton College Prep School, Bristol

My First Viking Raid

It was the year 823 and I was sailing across the North Sea in our Viking longship. It was my first raid and I was hoping I would do well. We had sailed for seven days until our first glimpse of land. We pulled onto the beach and started our attack. The main target was the monastery, known as the jackpot. Normally, the monks are weak and refuse to attack but this was different. All the English were waiting, armed with weapons. We were forced to retreat. Some men died and I barely escaped with my life.

Amber Miller (10)
Clifton College Prep School, Bristol

The Quest

Knut returned from stealing. He had stolen and killed the most people, he got promoted to go on a quest to kill the Saxon king of Mercia. Knut felt honoured to be chosen. He got ready to sail the next morning. At the crack of dawn, he set sail across the sea to get to the shores of England. Knut hid his boat behind a rock and disguised himself as a Saxon. He crept behind the guards and threw a flaming torch at the king. Knut ruled the city and now he was the new leader, king of England.

Alex Lind (10)
Clifton College Prep School, Bristol

Thor And His Beloved Hammer

In the land of Asgard, Thor lost his hammer. He had looked everywhere for it. Thor had a sense that Loki had stolen it but he was the only one who could pick it up. He found Loki holding his beloved hammer. He threw it over the Bifrost! Thor flew and grabbed it. He smashed it on the Bifrost and cracked it. Loki fell, Thor tried to grab him but Loki let go. Thor was horrified. Even though Loki was evil, he was his brother. At least he had his hammer back!

Lara Poulsom (10)
Clifton College Prep School, Bristol

I Saw A Fight

There in the distance stood a beautiful figure. Was I really seeing a goddess or was I blind? The figure was wearing a marvellous green and blue dress. Her hair was golden with a red ribbon with frilled edges. Then there was sound as two voices were fighting. I clutched my hands and held my breath. I realised that the two voices came from Freya and Thor. I felt stunned, more than most people. My special, marvellous secret must never get out.

Libby Bullen (10)
Clifton College Prep School, Bristol

Secrets

'Today, Victoria, you will be learning how to look after the garden,' said Butler Bross. When Victoria heard the butler shout to her, she got up and ran downstairs. When Victoria was learning how to sow the seeds, she got very hot.

Her mother said, 'Go get a drink from the mountain river.'

As she went around the corner, she couldn't see a thing, only smoke. She waved her hands across her mouth to get the smoke away. As the smoke cleared, she found a boy who was from Egypt. She kept this a secret from her brother, Danny.

Brogan Meehan (10)
Ditcham Park School, Petersfield

The Unfortunate Child

Today was the day I died. I woke up to find two Aztec men, I was puzzled about what they said. 'Come with us, you have been chosen to become a sacrifice,' they whispered in unison. They dragged me away to the temple, they made me stride up the stairs.

I tripped and fell so they hauled me up to the bloody, sacrificial stone. There I saw a dark figure with a jagged jewel-encrusted dagger. The two men pushed me down on the stone, a dark figure came, the knife dropped down. *Squelch!* I saw my throbbing heart...

Jack Keeping (10)
Ditcham Park School, Petersfield

Behind You!

I was fighting against the Spanish army, running around in the pit of dead warriors, my armour clanking and clashing about. *I need to sit down*, I thought, but I wouldn't give up now! I started fighting against another Spanish warrior. 'Argh! Ouch! Grrr!' I yelled as each wound appeared on my bare skin. Our swords clattered and crashed. I got him right across the face and he fell to his hands and knees.

'Behind you!' yelled a voice out in the distance. The last thing I saw was a metal blade being plunged into my sweating, trembling body!

Jemima Butler (10)
Ditcham Park School, Petersfield

Sacrifice

I am walking up the steps to the top, to be sacrificed. My legs shaking, my arms trembling. One step from the top I hear a very familiar voice. It is my extremely annoying husband. He says, 'My sweet, loving wife, I will be sacrificed instead of you!' We both look at the priest, hoping he will say yes. The priest does allow this to happen so I start to walk down the steps, as happy as a bird.
It happens. My husband is gone forever. No more annoying talk. This is the best day of my whole, entire life.

Annie Rowley (10)
Ditcham Park School, Petersfield

The Sacrifice

It was a burning-hot day, especially for me, a prisoner about to die in a horrid way. The priest was going to slice my chest and rip out my heart. I was petrified. When I got to the top of the temple, I was even more frightened. I was so stupid for letting them take me away. I walked over to the sacrificial stone, then I saw the priest walking over, he said, 'For your sacrifice, just for company a god will watch you die!'
'Argh!' The last thing I saw was blood everywhere and an evil god.

Daniela Dobby (10)
Ditcham Park School, Petersfield

The Darkness Has Come...

As I stumble up these treacherous stairs, I think, *This is my destiny*. I am honoured to be a sacrifice to my Aztec gods. I will keep them happy, repay them well. I can hear them bellow, 'We are ready to kill!' with a smirk.

Is this the end? Is it the beginning? How will I know? Is this really what my terrified soul tells me to do? Shall I do it? I feel their wrinkly, sweaty hands holding me down. I have seen my last sight and now I see only darkness.

Will Goldmann (10)
Ditcham Park School, Petersfield

Pompeii

The emperor strutted into the theatre of Pompeii, his laurel wreath covering his shameful baldness. His snow-white robe drooped from his shoulders. He sat down in deafening silence. He sluggishly bowed his head. The crowd sat down, except one gang of grizzly, unshaven men. Swiftly, they pounced like jaguars. Their knives glimmered in the sun. Their weapons plunged into Caesar's skull. He collapsed from his chair but knives still came raining down. His corpse was writhing violently, in a vast pool of his own blood. The crowd screamed in pure terror and ran. Caesar had slowly perished in pain.

Jake Last (10)
Ditcham Park School, Petersfield

Oopsy Daisy

Zolin and Timmy were running across the hard brick path, alongside the pebbly road, towards the fresh-smelling Sunday market. The market sold homemade bread, lovely milk, delicious muffins and millions of other things in little white sheds. Some days the priests came to buy bread for the slaves. Zolin and Timmy were running so fast, Zolin accidentally stepped on the priest's foot. Zolin didn't realise that he had done it so he carried on. Suddenly a loud voice shouted, 'I have found the first sacrifice, come now to the tower of sacrifice,' he said in a low, dark voice.

Hattie Cobden (10)
Ditcham Park School, Petersfield

Thief

As Alexander entered the Colosseum, fear etched his dark blue eyes and tears streamed down his face. He cautiously looked around and happened to find the emperor, a smile was playing across his wrinkly face. In the emperor's mind, Alexander was just a thief, a dirty, preposterous, lying thief, guilty of stealing an apple. The emperor's corrupt mind had decided to kill Alexander here in the arena, fully equipped with iron armour, sword and shield, like a gladiator. Alexander did not stand a chance against the lion. The gates creaked open to reveal the dark, crimson eyes...

Jake Jones (10)
Ditcham Park School, Petersfield

The Beaches Of Britain

Julius Caesar rode onto the beach, legionnaires following behind, the sound of arrows slicing through the air. Then there were screams of terror. Caesar saw Celts, this was not the first time Caesar killed Celts. He'd taken Gaul from Celts, he could take another country. The Celts marched onto the beach with bows, arrows, swords, clubs, shields and chariots, but the legionnaires ran up the beach as Celts ran down. Now the battle really started and then the sound of death roared over the battlefield. Romans ruthlessly killed Celts and Celts killed Romans.

Miles Barber (10)
Ditcham Park School, Petersfield

The Beast

1463, England, Romans. *Screech! Bang!* 'Nooo!' Then silence. The raiders had left the village. Jack and Zack woke up, they seemed rather puzzled because they were in a boat with guards surrounding them. Zack looked at them again and he had a funny feeling that they were the raiders - he was right! *Thwack!* They were both knocked out. Zack woke up, shortly followed by Jack. The raiders grabbed them and threw them into the cage, where the Minotaur lived. They were both given an iron sword and together they slayed the Minotaur.

Freddie Lock (10)
Ditcham Park School, Petersfield

Tomalulla Gets Sacrificed...

As I, Winstozuma, watched that pitiful slave, Tomalulla, climb up the pyramid steps, I started to think about the slave. He was badly overworked and was trembling as he climbed up the staircase. I almost started feeling bad for him. Tomalulla was getting closer to the top now. I felt the obsidian sacrificial knife in my hand. Very soon I would have to strike it down on Tomalulla's body. Tomalulla was now laid down on the bloodstained altar with two priests holding him down. I raised the knife high above my head. I then struck the knife down...

Winston Smith (10)
Ditcham Park School, Petersfield

Beast Battle

In Rome, in a magnificent palace, sat Julius Caesar with a knife, with his Roman shield, golden chest plate and leggings. He walked in the lounge, a beast was tearing up the room. Luckily, Julius Caesar battled the beast. Julius killed the beast by stabbing the beast through the heart when he wasn't looking. Blood poured everywhere! With the dead carcass, they served up a blood tea. Slaves made the carcass into beast burgers and all the poor people in the kingdom were fed. Then he fed all the Roman army too. They ate until they fell asleep!

Joseph Handley (9)
Ditcham Park School, Petersfield

Annie

Annie put on her favourite dress for Shakespeare's new play at the Globe Theatre. Once everyone was seated, the play began. The crowd was silent. Annie started kicking the seat in front of her. The man next to the seat she was kicking whispered, 'Stop!' but soon enough, she was doing it again. This time the person in front turned around - oh no! It was Henry VIII! Henry grabbed Annie and took her to a dark room where hundreds of axes were hanging on the wall. He hung one over Annie's head and, *chop!* It was gone!

Amelia Taee (9)
Ditcham Park School, Petersfield

Pyramid Water

Where is it? I know it's here somewhere, hundreds of people get lost in this temperature. Where is that well? I walk and come across an enormous pyramid, it has stunning swirly patterns all over. I run my fingers along the polished wall. A doorway opens, stairs twist up into the starless night. It seems to hypnotise me into walking up and I enter a room with different tombs scattered around the floor. Suddenly, the floor starts to shake. I ran as fast as I can down the stairs, the doorway has sealed. I slowly enter my death-life.

Hatty Wood (10)
Ditcham Park School, Petersfield

The Guillotine...

I crumple at Marius' feet, gulping air. Amelie scans the area, we are safe, for now. We hear the stamping of feet and there are shouts for blood. My blood runs cold, my entire body stiffens with terror. Amelie pulls me to my feet, but she is too late, the guards are surrounding us, Marius has been tied to a post and Amelie has been taken away from me - her screams vibrate around the dark alleyway. I am dragged away from them both, forever... I plummet to my knees and obediently bow my head, the blade plunges.

Qetsiah Joachim-Baggott (9)
Ditcham Park School, Petersfield

The Battle Of The Dinosaurs

Rex was incredibly hungry and there was absolutely no food in sight so he stomped up to a triceratops and ate it. At lunchtime, Rex tiptoed up to Spine's territory and started to attack. Spine was startled by this and began to attack too. Spine took an immense bite of Rex and he collapsed but Rex was still active so he fought on the ground. It was a death that took two days. Once the battle was over, Spine ate him. Spine loved the meat so much he wanted to trample on Rex's territory and eat the T-rexes.

Finn Lewis (9)
Ditcham Park School, Petersfield

Dick Turpin

I started out as a Georgian butcher, when I came across a gang of robbers called the Greggory Gang. We roamed around Essex, murdering and robbing in daylight. Finally the Greggory Gang got caught. The gang was probably executed but I escaped. I ran away to Yorkshire and changed my name to John Palmer. I was sent to jail for stealing chickens. I sent a letter to my family but the postman had taught me how to write, so he went to the police and they had me hung. My name was Dick Turpin, the highway man.

Oliver Osgood (9)
Ditcham Park School, Petersfield

A Summer Aztec Death

On a hot, humid summer's day in Tenochtitlan, I stood in front of a massive Aztec temple, about to come face-to-face with an obsidian knife. I saw the steps I'd been dreading in front of me. I took a deep breath and started nervously climbing the steps, towards my end. As I came closer to the top, I remembered my family back where I lived, I had to keep strong. I reached the top, I saw the priest waiting for me. As I laid on the stone, I thought, *The better world has come at last.*

Harry Soden-Bridger (10)
Ditcham Park School, Petersfield

Untitled

It was a baking-hot day, me and my friends were playing football as normal. I heard a roar, I knew it wasn't good. Everyone ran for their lives. I stayed. I wanted to see what was making that noise. I saw trees being smashed up in the woods. I saw a head through the gaps in the leaves. It scanned for its next victims: my friends. They were still running and screaming as loudly as they could. It came bounding after them, they would never outrun it! In the blink of an eye, they were gone.

Matthew Saunders (10)
Ditcham Park School, Petersfield

My Last Breath

The rain powers down and the lightning crashes. I hide behind the tree, catch my breath, but I can hear the beast howling. He is coming. I run until I have lost my breath, but I can see his red eyes coming. I'm shaking now, I have legs of jelly and it feels as if I could fall over anytime soon. All I can think is, *Somebody save me!* The trees are hard to dodge, my foot catches on a root. I fall. The Minotaur is here. As he jabs his teeth into me, I steal my last breath.

Cecily Brown (9)
Ditcham Park School, Petersfield

The Day I Died!

As I walked up the bloody temple steps, sparkling with wet, fresh blood, a surge of fear overcame me. For today was the day I was due to be sacrificed. A huge crowd had formed to watch me die. As I reached the top, a huge surge of terror overcame me as I saw the other people being sacrificed. Soon it was my turn and as I laid down, I could hear the crowd shouting below me. I could see the priest pulling out the bloody dagger. He raised it and the last thing I saw was my heart!

Tom Duddridge (10)
Ditcham Park School, Petersfield

The Treasure Of The Beast

Once upon a time, there was a boy called James. He was fifteen years old and and his family was very poor. James went for a walk one day and found a cave. At the bottom of the cave was a lot of treasure. James went down into the cave and got the treasure. When he got back home, James hid it in his closet. The owner of the treasure was the most terrifying beast in the world. He would do anything to get his treasure. So he went to get his treasure. He did get the treasure!

Theo Cable (10)
Ditcham Park School, Petersfield

Why Me?

I was walking up the stairs of the temple. I saw the Aztec priest at the top with a knife in his hand and a grin on his face. He already had blood on it from the last sacrifice. The whole of my body was trembling, my heart was pumping so fast I nearly passed out. But then I looked on the bright side. If I died it would make the world go on. When I got to the top, the priest made me put my body on a bloody stone, then he lifted up a knife - 'Nooo!' *Crunch!*

Sebastian Hopkins (10)
Ditcham Park School, Petersfield

An Unexpected Ending...

First, I was wondering around Mongolia, then I was being chased by a huge creature! I ran and ran like my life depended on it. Probably because it did. I had to start running on all fours. It got closer and tried to bite me, kill me. I looked back and made eye contact. Its bloodshot eyes looked straight at me. I looked forward and nearly smashed straight into a tree. It bent down and tried to eat me. It tripped and broke its neck. I, a velociraptor, had defeated a T-rex.

George Henderson (10)
Ditcham Park School, Petersfield

They Are Here!

There was a knock at the door. It was then I remembered what was going to happen. I didn't dare open the door, but there was no need, they barged through and picked me up. I screamed as loud as I could, the pain was agonising, they took me and Pa to a colossal temple in Tenochtitlan. The Aztec priest was waiting at the top. Walking to the top was like climbing a mountain to the gods. At the top, there was a rack of skulls. A big grey stone was waiting for me...

Francesca Walmsley (10)
Ditcham Park School, Petersfield

The Missing Sun

Ra the sun god had finished breakfast and was sitting in his garden. 'Julie,' he called into a crate. A gigantic dung beetle came out, licking its lips as the breakfast it had eaten was very crunchy. Ra picked up Julie and said, 'Bigem!' Before their eyes, Julie grew. Ra unhooked the giant gas ball and passed it to Julie. As she soared away, pushing the ball, Ra returned to his seat and unfogged the glass gazing ball. He could see Julie soaring joyfully up to the Heavens. Suddenly, clouds blocked the view. When they cleared, Julie had disappeared.

Maizy Day (10)
Downs Junior School, Brighton

Roman Diary Of A Young Slave Girl

Somewhere in Rome, there was a young girl called Damitilla. One day she was walking down the street, she saw people walking. She went next to them and they captured her! As she opened her eyes, she was dressed in a white dress, the same as slaves. She stood up and went through the hall, where she saw two people - one boy and a girl. They said, 'Hello, can you clean up our rooms, please?'

'OK,' Damitilla said. She went upstairs to their bedrooms. As she went inside, she saw an open door. She went outside and ran away!

Dana Aben (10)
Dragon School, Oxford

When Nobody Believed In The Plague...

'I'm telling you, I'm telling you...'
This all started when my mother died. She was such a kind person, always excited to see everybody, even if they weren't the greatest of friends. Anyway, the day she died was shocking. From that day on, my dad and I went around telling everybody about the plague. They took us to court for scaring people and putting up too many posters. It would mean ten years in jail! Too many people had died already, they had to face the facts... 'I'm telling you...'

Alexander Phelps (9)
Dragon School, Oxford

Think Before You Do

Back and forth, the longship swung in time with the waves.

'Bone-Breaker!' screamed Captain Crusher.

Breaker dived in front of Crusher's nose. 'Yes, Captain?'

The captain pushed Bone-Breaker back, disgusted by his breath. 'Make this slave walk the wooden plank!'

Very sheepishly, Breaker did as he was told and moments later, Carl, the slave, found himself at the end of what he thought was a line of string. 'Mr Bone-Breaker, you don't have to do this. Inside your heart, deep down, you are an amazing person.'

Breaker hesitated before jumping onto the plank. 'What have I done?'

Ciara O'Neill (10)
Farringtons Junior School, Chislehurst

The Nasty Vikings

Once there was a little boy called Fredy. He was very educational and shy. His father, Grave Beard, and his best friend, Tabala, were planning to attack the coast of England. It was known as a very wealthy and rich country. Tabala took all the boats and handed them to a captain. Fredy exclaimed nervously, 'Don't tell me you meant me to be a captain!' But he became a captain, and soon they attacked England. They killed every person and left skin shreds everywhere. There was blood on the trees and grass. The Vikings had won!

Maria Manta (11)
Farringtons Junior School, Chislehurst

Anglo-Saxons Vs Vikings

The waves roared, the sky was grey, lightning struck. As I gazed into the distance, I saw a long, narrow Viking ship. I summoned my army but as we gathered our weapons, we were too late! The Vikings had already arrived, they jumped out of their boats and slashed almost half the army! I was petrified, I sprinted for my life. As I ran out of breath, a Viking stood over me and held up his sharp axe. I knew right at that second that the Vikings had won. This was the day I died, or so I thought.

Nicki Kardel
Farringtons Junior School, Chislehurst

The Viking Raid

I, a young boy born in AD 800, am sitting on the edge of a cliff, scanning the horizon for Dad's ship. After waiting hours, I see a tiny dot move closer and closer. I jump for joy. Minutes pass, it's moving too fast; the drum beat is wrong, it's full of anger. I need to hide, it's now dark. I silently climb out of the well, nothing is moving. They've taken everything. The only thing that the Vikings have left is our broken hearts.

Flo Benfield (10)
Georgeham CE Primary School, Braunton

Ashley And Abigail The Victorians

'Where am I?' Abigail spluttered as the sharp, cobbles dug into her back.

'Welcome to Dusty Street!' a voice came behind her, 'I'm Ashley, and you are?'

'Abigail.'

'Nice to meet you, Abigail, where do you live?'

'I don't know,' Abigail sobbed. One cold tear ran down her face, it stuck to her cheek and froze because of the cold air.

'It's OK,' Ashley said, 'you can stay at my house!'

'Really?'

'Of course! You can be my best friend!' The tear shattered and Abigail's cheeks became rosy. The two best friends in Victorian times lived happily.

Isabella Blundell (10)
Great Tew Primary School, Chipping Norton

Untitled

Murmurs spread across the crowd as they were about to watch the execution of Prince Rupert. Loads of people gathered around to watch and cheer.

Two days before, people gathered around in a room to discuss the fate of Prince Rupert. 'Traitor!' someone shouted. Everyone murmured when the decision was made to execute Prince Rupert. Prince Rupert was dragged up to the podium with a cloth round his head because he knew the executioner. The person doing the execution might have tried to stop it happening.

Hattie Souch (11)
Great Tew Primary School, Chipping Norton

Untitled

I am walking through the cold, dusty, dark halls of a
pyramid. I stand on a stone and the wall slides
across. It is a secret room. The biggest room in the
pyramid. I walk in, with a scared look on my face.
A couple of minutes later, I hear a moan as a
mummy rises from the biggest coffin. The mummy
looks around and then sees me. It doesn't look
happy. The next thing I know, the mummy is
chasing me back through the dusty halls of the
pyramid. 'Run!' he moans, so I do.

Sophie Wilson-Fry (10)
Great Tew Primary School, Chipping Norton

Plane

Johnathan and Charles are brothers who were inspired by battles when they were growing up. They went training to fly their planes one day, the Air Chief Marshall had called everyone together. There was a war. Johnathan was the first to jump into his plane. He was excited and charged, he was also the best pilot in the squadron. They took off and were just flying around when Charles' plane shuttered. *Bang!* Johnathan had spotted an enemy plane - it was dark and Charles was dropping off. His plane tilted to the ground, that was the end, for now.

Finlay Beggin (11)
Great Tew Primary School, Chipping Norton

World War One

They were coming. Gunshots fired and tanks destroyed everything in their path. There was no turning back. Sweat slowly dripped down my neck as I took my first shot. *Drip, drip.* Suddenly, my mind turned to my family; my eyes flooded with tears, I fell into the bottomless trench. I felt weak and useless, I didn't want to do this anymore. I looked up to the sky, it wasn't the bright, sunny day that it used to be, it was dark, cloudy and full of smoke. But then a beam of light shone and a football came out of nowhere.

Jamie Levene (11)
Great Tew Primary School, Chipping Norton

Trapped

I felt my way around the forbidden cave. My mouth stone-dry, my voice was hoarse with shouting. No one came. I was alone, abandoned. I scrambled around in the mud. In the distance, I heard a faint voice echoing, 'Hello!' I opened my mouth as my heart filled with glee, ready to shout my response. Nothing came out. I had no voice, my one chance slipped away from me. I banged on the stone walls of my prison in despair. I heard a small clatter as a rock fell to the floor. A small light pierced my eyes. Hope!

Blythe Ferguson (10)
Great Tew Primary School, Chipping Norton

Typhon Broke Out

He easily broke out, smashing everything in his path. He was coming and he was angry. The gods charged, every single one except Poseidon, he was in his own war. Typhon flicked the gods away like rag dolls, he was almost to Olympus, the gods were all injured. He furiously stomped over a flowing stream and the water amazingly drained his energy. He exploded into yellow dust and went back to Tartarus. It was Poseidon. Hopefully, he'd never be able to take a form again. Mount Etna was peaceful from then on.

Reuben Anthony (9)
Great Tew Primary School, Chipping Norton

Untitled

What had I done? What was I thinking? I never thought they'd catch me out, this was not supposed to happen. As I walked along the dusty track, everyone passing me gave me a stern stare, making me feel uncomfortable. I arrived home, I was cold and hungry and had no money. Cheating in the Olympics had given me a hard life lesson and I knew that I would never do it again. I went to get some water and on my way I collapsed, I couldn't make it any further. The lights turned off and everything was gone.

Matilda Mackie (10)
Great Tew Primary School, Chipping Norton

Sarah On The Battlefield

I couldn't stop, not now. I needed to bandage up a few more men, then I could finish and stop. After about thirty minutes of dodging bullets, I made my way to a suffering man in agony; he had lost his leg. I quickly bandaged it up and dragged him to a heap of mud for shelter. Bullets rained. I suddenly realised the man had closed his eyes. I shouted at him, but he didn't respond. I knew he was dead. I stopped there, waiting in shock. Then a drip of blood fell onto my arm. I was dead!

Gethin Collins (11)
Great Tew Primary School, Chipping Norton

First But Last

The word 'go' echoed throughout my head as we started running. I overtook the man in front of me. There was no one in front of me anymore. I was first. I could feel the sweat running down my head. My legs were in pain but I needed to carry on. I could see the finish line on the horizon. This was the moment I had been training ten months for. I could hear the crowd roaring as I ran towards the finish line, right in front of me now. Suddenly, I tripped over a rock and the others finished.

Victoria Louro (11)
Great Tew Primary School, Chipping Norton

Untitled

Bob, the stupid explorer, was not so stupid after all. He had found the treasure! Carrying his treasure, he ran out of the pyramids. He could see the shadows of the dead pharaohs running after him. Bob's boot got stuck in the sand and one of the pharaoh's mummy's arms came flying through the air with the boot. The boot hit Bob! Bob fell to the ground with a thud. When the pharaoh's mummies tried to pick up the treasure, they fell to pieces. The treasure vanished! Stupid Bob!

Archie Leigh-Wood (10)
Great Tew Primary School, Chipping Norton

The Chop

Some say my lips still whispered - praying - I'm not too sure, I wasn't there to see it. I remember it like it was yesterday. They were huddled in a circle around me, a dark hooded figure stood in front of me with a gleaming axe in their hands. Knowing that soon that axe would not be so clean sent chills down my spine. How could he do this to me? I married Henry thinking he'd treat me well. As the shimmering axe came towards me, I knew this was it, but I'd get him back.

Scarlet Floyd (11)
Great Tew Primary School, Chipping Norton

Burning

All I could see was darkness, I could feel that it made my throat tickle then break into sudden coughs, I could feel the sweat starting on my forehead. Then my raggedy, old, battered clothes stuck to me. I heard monstrous Martin and Mr McGumary bellow my name. 'Get up there, unwanted!' Then I heard laughing and all my hope was lost. I saw smoke, I looked down - I was forbidden to look down - but this was an emergency. I saw fire burning so brightly and I knew that was it.

Eliza Carleton Paget (11)
Great Tew Primary School, Chipping Norton

Unexpected Guests

I climbed the tree. Having fun, I looked out to the horizon, then it all changed. I heard gunfire and the screams of my loved ones. The village was burnt to dust. A flame caught my dress. I jumped, I was falling, falling. I grabbed onto a vine, barely holding on. A man with pale skin looked at me. These were the people who killed my family. He pointed his gun at me. If I jumped, I'd die. If I stayed, I'd die... *Bang!*

Amber Owen (9)
Great Tew Primary School, Chipping Norton

Hot Coals

Master J Smith boomed so loudly the windowpanes shattered. 'Get to work,' he yelled at Billy, so Billy quickly clambered up the chimney and started sweeping the dusty black soot wildly. Then he started to feel really hot and sweaty, the sweat dripped down his face and suddenly he realised that Lady Clara, owner of the large manor house, had lit the hot coals! Billy knew that this was the end!

Jennifer Tambini-Aylett (11)
Great Tew Primary School, Chipping Norton

The Black Death

Today was the day they arrived; big ones, small ones, smelly rats. They terrorised children. Every day, more rats arrived by boat, spreading more diseases. The next day, my eyes were slowly closing, silently. Then it went black. Was I dead? Was it a dream? I was dead.

Archie Grant (9)
Great Tew Primary School, Chipping Norton

The Final Conflict

Clink! Slash! Bang! The two clans collided fiercely. We'd been at war with these filthy rats for the past week and today our leader, King Tristan, was determined to destroy them once and for all. I was cabin boy, supplying weapons for the crew. I wished I could fight and knock the crown of whoever was the king of the other side. Galahad ran past me, swearing and cursing as he did. He mentioned something that gave me an idea. I hastily abandoned my position as cabin boy, then I fired a cannon at the other ship. We won!

Roy Quartey (11)
Oasis Academy Long Cross, Bristol

World War Two

Sirens went off. People shut their curtains. Lights went off. The Germans were there. Bombs had been dropped over London. Everyone had rushed out to their Anderson shelters; it was safe. A small family were rushing through their back garden, trying not to be seen. 'When will it be over?' moaned the little girl called Mary.

'Soon, hopefully,' replied the mother, Mrs Wilson. They all sat and talked about how horrible it was being in the war.

'I hate the war! Germany and England should be at peace!' said Anne.

The next day, Mr Wilson went to war, children evacuated.

Imogen Davies (10)
Oasis Academy Long Cross, Bristol

Lonely Henry

'Yay! Henry and Jess are now married. Three cheers for the new queen.'
'Hip hip hooray! Hip hip hooray! Hip hip hooray!' cheered the crowd.
One year later, Jess died after giving birth to the heir to the throne, Henry's beloved child, Prince Alexander IX. Henry was devastated. His favourite wife, he was going to let live, had lost her mortal life. Henry, for once without a wife, walked around his castle as lonely as ever.
A few years later, Henry got married to another woman. Henry lived a happy life, knowing that someone, finally, loved him back.

Michael Court (11)
Oasis Academy Long Cross, Bristol

The Fiery Miracle...

Crackle! The sound of fire boomed and echoed throughout the house. Thomas, who was eight, was in his room playing with his brand-new toy. He was so mesmerised by it that he didn't notice the ear-splitting sound.

'Quickly, everyone out!' Thomas's father screeched. As they swiftly scampered out, they remembered Thomas. His father tried to get inside, but the fire was too close. Some people noticed this horrendous scene and said to make a human ladder. They grabbed Thomas's hand and heaved him down.

'Hooray!' they cheered. Thomas was saved and everyone thought it was a fiery miracle.

Nayeema Akther (11)
Oasis Academy Long Cross, Bristol

The Black Death

Once, in 1665, thee was a doctor called Steve, he was the plague doctor. In the morning, the doctor got dressed in a thick leather coat and a beak face mask that covered his face. Steve placed strong herbs in his mask so he wouldn't smell anything. Thirty minutes later, he went outside. He stepped outside and stepped in green mess. 'Yuck!' Steve strolled down the street and heard someone scream.
'Am... am I OK?' gasped Tom, who was Steve's best friend ever. Tom would die!

Kieran Cotterill (11)
Oasis Academy Long Cross, Bristol

Lonely Henry

Once, in Tudor times, there was a king called Henry. Henry loved getting married, he had usually divorced them or beheaded them, but sometimes they just died. He was bored so he wanted another wife. Henry searched and searched but no one was found. He did find someone but she looked like a horse.

After an hour of searching, Henry approached a young girl called Eve. Eve was only twenty-two, Henry was older at thirty-two. Eve was talking to him for an hour and then Henry asked Eve to marry him. He was rejected. He was still very lonely.

Mason Pike (11)
Oasis Academy Long Cross, Bristol

The Unknown Illness

The sun shone brightly as my two-year-old brother, Jack, and I took our carriage to London. We were going to visit our grandparents for two weeks. As we arrived, I felt a sudden chill down my spine. We came to a dark part of the village, Jack snuggled into me as we came closer and closer to the small, wooden cottage. Slowly, the carriage stopped. Jack and I went inside. The hut was silent.
After three days without our grandparents, Jack became ill. Then he started hiding in the closet. I didn't know what happened. Jack died.

Isabelle Stinchcombe (10)
Oasis Academy Long Cross, Bristol

The Great Fire Of London

As the moon shone brightly, an eerie silence filled the city.

The next morning, some of the people in London went into the bakery and got some breakfast. When everyone had gone, Niomi had a fiery bun, dropped it on the floor and set the floor on fire. In just a second, the fire spread onto the next house and kept on spreading, everyone was scared. The fire people came and had to get a lot of water from the River Thames with a leather bucket. They ran back to the houses and chucked water onto them.

Holly McCarthy (11)
Oasis Academy Long Cross, Bristol

He's Gone...

Whoooooop! The deafening sirens screeched through the fearful city of London. Desperate cries and yelps of families rang depressingly through the mildewed streets; the Germans were coming. My family and I cowered into our shelter, terrorised and frightened. Hours and hours of dreadful guns and wailing bombs made the innocent city distraught. Finally, the riot stopped and the town fell deathly silent. Shaken people crawled out of their shelters and choked and spluttered in the thick dust. A postman arrived with a battered letter from the Air Force. My heart froze painfully as I opened it. It couldn't be true...

Isabelle Howie (11)
Oasis Academy Long Cross, Bristol

Behind The Fire

The wonderful-smelling bakery sat beyond my house. A mouth-watering scent floated gracefully through the bustling city. I was starving; I haven't had anything to eat for the past few days. I didn't have any money. However, I was still going to try. As quick as lightning, I ran past the bakery, taking a piece of bread and knocking over the oven. The blazing fire danced viciously. The smell of burning wood tickled my nose. I could hear people screaming and saving all their possessions from the fire. I couldn't believe this was all my fault...

Natalia Gnatowicz (11)
Oasis Academy Long Cross, Bristol

Untitled

There it was! Staring with the sign of starvation in its wide eyes, blinking slightly. My heart stopped, my eyes widened. As it took a step forward, the trees shook. I dropped everything and raced for my life. I ran through the huge trees, towering down on me. The beast opened its immense jaw and let out an ear-piercing roar! Every time it stamped, I jumped in the air. Its long, sharp claws embedded in the damp mud, leaving enormous holes in the ground. I gave up. I just stood there, clenched my fists and squeezed my sapphire eyes together.

Regan O'Connor (11)
Oasis Academy Long Cross, Bristol

Mummy Trouble!

I sprinted down the long, narrow path. The shadow followed me everywhere I went. Right now, I couldn't stop; something was chasing me. It was pitch-black and I couldn't see a thing. Suddenly, silence filled the air. I felt like I was going to collapse onto the cold floor. I carried on walking; would you want to be caught by a mysterious beast? As I walked through the thin door, I saw a tall, majestic shadow. Suddenly, the footstep began again. I held my breath and walked out. There was no escape. I was in some mummy trouble...

Courteney Mazur (11)
Oasis Academy Long Cross, Bristol

Fire Started In London

The fire started! People began shouting. 'Gather water from the River Thames!' My mother woke me up as the ceiling began falling. I had no chance to move as it fell between my mother and myself. Fire rose, the wind turned into a hurricane. The fire came closer towards me and the open window. I jumped through the window. A stranger caught me. I ran with my mother but she lost her energy and fell into the fire. I dragged her and extinguished her. We ran to the countryside. We escaped the fire. I was a hero from burning London...

Joanna Milkiewicz (11)
Oasis Academy Long Cross, Bristol

Untitled

Zoom! Holy Zeus soared over the Greek village in his chariot of gold. The villagers cried out with praise, but I stayed in, for I hated Zeus. I hated him; he cast me down into the Underworld and I had been plotting my revenge ever since. I'm Hades, the feared God of the Underworld. Just because I rule the dead, people hate me! If they got to know me, I can be pretty awesome. So please, if you're reading this, spread the word - it gets pretty lonely. Please, I need some friends. Help me for once, please.

Fynnlay Booker (11)
Oasis Academy Long Cross, Bristol

The Great Fire

Once, a little boy called Dave woke up to see that his house was on fire so he quickly ran outside. He watched his small house collapse. When he turned around, he saw that the rest of the street wasn't there anymore. It was just rubble, all of the rubble was wood and glass. Dave had no parents left, they burnt to death in the fire. He thought to himself, *My grandma and grandad are still alive.* So he set off to his grandparents' house. When he got to where the house was, there was nothing there, just rubble.

Stanley Scrivin (11)
Oasis Academy Long Cross, Bristol

The Dinosaur Chase

He snuck through the colossal, tall forest. Trees covered the land. No light was seen. He walked around the corner when, suddenly, the floor shook. From around the corner, a head appeared. It was covered in scales and blood. Its teeth were sharp. It was a dinosaur! It loudly roared and started to run towards the man. He ran for his life. Sweat dripped down his face. He thought he had escaped when he ran into a hut. However, he was wrong. Claws stuck through the door, along with a hand and a huge head. There was no escape...

Louise Thomas (11)
Oasis Academy Long Cross, Bristol

The Great Fire Of London

Zac was hungry so he decided to cook something, but it took too long. He went down to the market and he forgot that he left his stove on. His sister was still at home. She just got out of the tin bath and she noticed the kitchen was on fire! Zac came home and saw Emily trying to put out the fire. The fire spread next door where Zoe and Harry lived. They ran out of the house and warned the other people in the village. They gathered water, then chucked it over their houses. The fire was gone.

Jade Checketts (10)
Oasis Academy Long Cross, Bristol

The 'Great' Fire!

The wind howled as a fire was ablaze. I escaped my house just in time, however, all of my possessions were destroyed. The streets were balls of fire and everyone was panicking; they didn't know what to do. As I looked into the distance, I saw the roof of St Paul's Cathedral melting in the inferno. We hastily ran, followed by a crowd towards the centre of London. We had jumped into the River Thames. We would be safe, or that's what we thought...

Harrison Bishop (11)
Oasis Academy Long Cross, Bristol

The Kings In New York City

Lola is in New York and she loves it. Suddenly, she sees something.

'What is that?' asks Lola. They are Vikings, four of them.

'We are here,' said Bob, one of the Vikings. Lola was so scared she could've cried.

'What do you want to do?' asked Arthur.

'I do not know,' said Jeff.

'Who are you?' asked Lola.

'We are the Vikings,' said the Vikings.

'Are you nice Vikings?' asked Lola.

'Yes,' said Tom.

'Do you want to go to Times Square?' said Lola.

'OK,' said the Vikings, so they all had fun at Times Square.

Mya Dinning (10)
Pitton CE Primary School, Salisbury

Moving On

It's 1941, I'm standing on the platform, gripping my mother's hand, butterflies in my stomach, waiting for the train to take George and I to the countryside. All I can think of are bombs crashing down, destroying my house. My heart beats faster as the train pulls slowly into the station.
'All evacuees board the train!' shouts the station master.
'Bye sweetie,' says Mother.
'No Mother, I don't want to leave you, please!'
'Darling, you have to!'
'No! I won't!' I scream.
'George take her,' she says, starting to cry.
'No Mother!' I shriek being dragged onto the train.
'Mother!'

Amy Puryer (11)
Pitton CE Primary School, Salisbury

Bear Attack Survivor

'Argh!' James yelled. His hand, where was it? He screamed. It was in the bear's mouth! He drew his sword. *Slash!*

'Roar!' It dropped dead. It was over.

As James ran down to the beach, he saw a boat on the horizon. *Oh!* he thought, *The Vikings!* He strolled on. He soon found a steep slope and at the top stood a Viking. 'I challenge you!' he yelled.

'OK!' James shouted.

'Go!' yelled the Viking. They began... *thud!*

'Ow!' Blood rushed out of James' new cut.

'Argh!' The Viking dropped dead. James spotted an adder moving silently through the grass.

Theo Evans (10)
Pitton CE Primary School, Salisbury

Bad Time For Engine Failure!

'Fuel, check, supply crates, check, engines, check, thrusters, check, good to go.' Alistor Conduit, the pilot of the Chempion spacecraft, was getting ready for the supply voyage to the BA Space Hotel.
'3... 2... 1... blast-off!'
'Reduce engine thrust now,' instructed Oliver Jenkins, the engineer.
'There's the space hotel, but isn't it drifting out of orbit?' said Luke Sycra.
'By golly, you're right, it's gone out of the 5,000 mile limit, its engines have failed. Pull alongside and nudge it back into orbit using magno-fusion clamps,' said Oliver.
'We did it, it's back in orbit!' said Matt. 'Hooray for us!'

Ruaridh Thomson Easter (10)
Pitton CE Primary School, Salisbury

The Fight At London

While I was in London, I heard some screaming and a bullet. Then, out on the horizon, I saw some silhouettes, getting closer and closer. I screamed! Then I saw it; the sea monster. 'Attack!' bellowed a voice. The boat got closer and so did the sea monster. 'My name is Penelope,' screamed the booming voice.

'Why hello there,' I said. *Bang!* Bullet shots echoed in my ears. On the horizon, a ship sank. Penelope was an ugly woman with warts all over her face.

'Katie, wake up!' called her brother.

'Katie!' shouted her mum.

Finally, she was wide awake.

Imogen Ryan (9)
Pitton CE Primary School, Salisbury

The Great Escape

'Argh!' yelled Charles in pain; Hitler was interrogating Charles, Jezza and Winston. Suddenly, the sirens went off. John assassinated one of the German guards and shouted, 'Evacuate the area!'

Then he took Jezza, Charles and Winston to a secret British bunker underground. He revealed himself.

'Who are you?' asked Charles.

'I'm British and I'm saving your life,' replied John. It was obvious he didn't feel like talking - no one knew what he was doing. Then he started walking away to what looked like a lifeboat. 'Climb in,' said John. They jumped into it. Where were they going?

Finn Bergstrom (10)
Pitton CE Primary School, Salisbury

The Figure

Silence hit the town, there was a black figure in the distance. Who is he? Where did he come from? 'I am King!' said the figure. 'I am your master,' said the figure again, 'you will bow and worship me, yes, you children as well!'
The mum screamed in horror. 'Run!' shouted a man, 'He has got an army with weapons and guns! Save your children and families. One man from every family, come and fight with me,' said the man.
'All of this love doesn't change a thing in my point of view, army. Kill!'
'This isn't the end!'

Evelyn Lush (11)
Pitton CE Primary School, Salisbury

The Chop

I put my head in the hole of the guillotine. I'm sweating, I can see my family crying, all I did was steal a loaf of bread from the bakers to feed my family. My heart is beating like a cheetah running. The executioner is winding up the rope. *Click!* 'Ready!' comes a voice, it is the executioner.
'Yes,' I say, slowly.
'All right then, off we go.' I take a deep breath in. *Chop!* I feel the blade hit my neck, blood squirting, my head drops and death crawls along. The end is near, I feel it.

Josh Key (10)
Pitton CE Primary School, Salisbury

Sherlock Holmes And The Case Of Jack's Ripper Streak

The radio was blaring while Sherlock Holmes read his paper. He was reading an article when he heard the radio booming, 'Ripper strikes again, woman killed outside pub!'

'Watson!' shouted Holmes with a mouthful of smoke. 'We've got a murder on our hands.'

Watson's cart turned up at the crime scene one hour later, to find a mangled clump, with blood as far as the eye could see. The person who did this left a knife next to the body. Watson was just about to step forward when a gunshot went off. Startled, Holmes' assistant fell! And the Ripper ran.

Oliver Chalke (11)

Pitton CE Primary School, Salisbury

Thief Hunter

As I ran through the woods, I could still hear the booming of Thor's voice, thundering about lost hammers and thieves. I followed the culprit's tracks until I came to a cave. Inside the deep, dark hideout was a dark tunnel. At the end of this puzzling passage, it opened out into a massive cavern. One word crossed my mind in those few seconds before the explosion: 'Thief!'
When I awoke, the thief was cowering by the entrance, her back to the door, terror in her face. *Thud! Thud! Thud!* The door broke open; splinters of fragmented wood flew everywhere...

Perran Akib (10)
Pitton CE Primary School, Salisbury

Beowolf: The Scourge Of Scotland

Years ago, there was a bloodthirsty creature that roamed the huge lands of Scotland. He terrorised villages and destroyed towns. King Vladimir of Scotland, however, sent a whole army of his men to defeat the terrible monster. The journey was long and almost a third of the army had fallen before they even got there. The battle lasted for days and even weeks.

The horrible creature was defeated by a brave, young knight called Sir Klinsman. A week later, they returned to the castle but in their excitement, they didn't notice that King Vladimir was dead and covered in blood!

Finn Sainsbury (10)
Pitton CE Primary School, Salisbury

The Evil Submarine

Jacob was full of joy until he pressed the wrong button. It was 'the exploding button'. So after that, Jacob's submarine turned evil, it was hunting down Jacob, but soon Jacob darted through the sea. Meanwhile, Jacob's submarine was slowing down, so Jacob was free! When Jacob's submarine got back its energy, the submarine started finding its prey - Jacob. Finally, Jacob found some rare seaweed to cure his submarine. After that, his submarine found him. It started again so Jacob had to outrun his submarine. Then he put the seaweed inside the submarine.

Alexandar Kadiev (9)
Pitton CE Primary School, Salisbury

The Escape

It was a busy day at Hampton Court. Henry VIII was having his 40th birthday. There were many Lords, Dukes and important people laughing, drinking and eating constantly. Mya entered with a tray of well-cooked meats. Henry kept shouting orders at her with anger. Mya rushed out of the room with tears in her eyes. She got to her room and decided to escape because the king wouldn't let her see her family. When she had packed, Mya rushed along the corridor and suddenly, the wall opened! Mya followed a secret passage that led her back to her loving family.

Daisy Acreman (11)
Pitton CE Primary School, Salisbury

War

Everything seemed to slow down, all the fighting and suffering. I couldn't hear anything but shouting and gunfire. Then it stopped. For a split-second everything was silent. Peace at last! One lone soldier started cheering, then another, and then another - soon it had spread like wildfire right across the Western Front. All the caps in the air looked like a flock of birds. Men on both sides got out of their trenches, shaking hands and thumping each other on their backs with pure joy, exchanging tales of the war. This was what peace felt like.

Ella Azzopardi (10)
Pitton CE Primary School, Salisbury

The First Raid

It was quiet and peaceful as I walked quickly through the park from work. I heard distant plane engines. Women screamed, shielding their children, men pushing their families into trees to try and protect them. I ran to find shelter, any at all. As I sprinted, I saw a struggling old couple. I went over and helped them to shelter. By now, explosions were going off, clouding my view, making me cough. That was the last thing I remembered before being woken to the sound of sirens and people moaning, groaning and weeping. The Blitz had begun!

Sophie Buxton (11)
Pitton CE Primary School, Salisbury

The Mythical Pheaonith

Climbing the vines of the mythical flying Island of Terror, Captain Grimlock and his crew wound up in a deep, dark forest. The Pheaonith was creeping up on them. 'Look out!' yelled one of the crew. *Swoosh!* The Pheaonith picked up one of the crew. As it carried them to its nest high in the mountain, they started to climb up the mountain. One of the crew fell off. The captain was alone. The captain quickly figured out where the nest was. He ran to save the one crew member but there was no one there!

Sean Parker (11)
Pitton CE Primary School, Salisbury

Friends

The bell rang for the end of laundry duties. Myself and the other girls trudged down the corridor for dinner. I would never forget Grace but deep down I saw it coming; influenza was so hard to cure. Once we were dismissed from the table, we went to the girls' dorm to change into our nightclothes. I blew out my candle and climbed into bed. It was now very late at night - I heard the door open, slowly. A white, transparent figure resembling Grace drifted through, it sent a chill down my spine. Yet, I wasn't afraid...

Jess Mossman-Smith (11)
Pitton CE Primary School, Salisbury

The Viking Invasion

The waves crashed against the rocks, we could see land, so no need to send the raven out. We were getting ready with our axes and guns to invade the town, then we jumped off the boat and shouted, 'Charge!' We all fired gunshots. There were loud screams coming from every direction. We sent monks on board the ship to be slaves. We travelled from city to city, country to country, then finally, what we had been waiting for all our lives - we captured every monk as a slave, conquered the world and celebrated!

William Horsfall (10)
Pitton CE Primary School, Salisbury

I'm The Witness!

As I walk deeper into the woods, I hear loud thumps on the ground, angry and ferocious. As I inch closer to the threatening noise, I hear a roar. I stay still, my heart freezes. I can hear the thumps and roars coming closer but I still remain standing silent in fear. Suddenly, this loud thump strikes my ear. I slowly turn around, trying not to make a single sound. In the blink of an eye, I'm face-to-face with an ugly beast! My heart stops and my mouth drops, knowing that I'm in trouble! A Minotaur!

Faith Hellyer (11)
Pitton CE Primary School, Salisbury

A Scary Surprise

I feel a warm breath on my neck. I turn to look, my head shaking continuously, my heart skips a beat. When I finally turn around, I'm face-to-face with a scary, angry monster who has sharp teeth and scales flowing down his back. I run as fast as I can, tripping over scattered twigs and rocks on the mud. I suddenly stop and so does the monster. When I look at him, his eyes are huge with tears and his evil face drops into a scared one. I walk up to the monster and stare in disbelief.

Ruby Mann (11)
Pitton CE Primary School, Salisbury

Attacking New York City

I was walking to work when I heard and felt the ground shaking. Then I saw what seemed to be a Transformer. I started to run to a Metro station to get cover. It came closer and I heard an explosion and people screaming. The police came down and told everyone to get onto a train to the next Metro station. The police asked me to come with them and I went in an army car and drove to an army base. They gave me some weapons and then told me to run outside and attack the Transformers!

Tomas Bozic (10)
Pitton CE Primary School, Salisbury

Vane Attack

'Vikings, Vikings!' I yelled as I grabbed my sword. 'Defend our home!' It was scary, so scary, this was the battle for Ramsgate. Scar and I were ready, standing with our friends.

'Ready, Salvar?' Scar asked me, reassuringly.

'As ready as ever,' I answered. We charged and fought to the end, it was only about ten minutes.

'We're winning!' I yelled to Scar.

'Those Vikings will never win,' said Scar happily.

'Ragnor, we must run!' yelled the Viking leader, Vane.

'Retreat,' Ragnor yelled. Every Viking left, fleeing to the boats from which they came. We had won this battle!

Charles Westby (10)
Ramsgate Holy Trinity CE (A) Primary School, Broadstairs

Riding In My Hot Air Balloon

It was time to bring out my beauty.
I call her Priceless.
I got in and rose to the sky! You have to have skill and passion to fly Priceless; but I could fly her whilst making a cup of Earl Grey tea!
My name is John Logsworth and I can spot a small factory and I hate it! Making kids risk their life and limbs for work, and that is horrid! I wasn't really taking any notice of Priceless and I think she was getting jealous because we were sinking down, down, down where I couldn't stop it...

Noah Shakeshaft (10)
Ramsgate Holy Trinity CE (A) Primary School, Broadstairs

Tsunami

I am Finn and my friend, Jack, and I are in Los
Angeles in 1980, on Muscle beach.
I am lifting weights when I see a
tsunami... 'Tsunami!' I yell.
Everyone runs except Jack who says, 'Good for
y...' then sees the huge wave. Jack and I dash into
a random guy's house. Water goes up to ankle
height. A TV explodes. It goes up to our knees, to
our chests. Then it goes above our mouths. We
gurgle. Then it goes over our heads. Bubbles form.
We scramble but that is when the bubbles stop.

Louis Benedict-Evans (10)
Ramsgate Holy Trinity CE (A) Primary School, Broadstairs

Cleopatra's Catastrophe

My journey back is exhausting. I am now coming over a sand dune and I see... my home! I am so excited to get into my bedroom. I race past my village, 'Cleopatra has arrived! says my cat. 'I have taken over and you will be my slave!' Everybody is bowing down to my cat! A gust of wind blows past my beautiful face.

'No!' I scream and my pet's eyes turn red with rage. Two people's dusty, dirty hands take my sparkling crown. The next thing I know is I'm locked up for 1,000 dreadful years.

Georgiana Michael
Ramsgate Holy Trinity CE (A) Primary School, Broadstairs

War Winners

There goes the siren, the Germans are here. Time to take-off in my Spitfire and soar higher and higher onto the battlefield. I've got a German bomber in my sights. *Boom!* A direct hit from my twin missiles. But what's that behind me? Two missiles? 'Argh! I've been hit. We are losing altitude. Mayday, Mayday.' *Crash!* I blacked out. However, I seem to have landed on...
Hitler?

Jack Welsh (9)
Ramsgate Holy Trinity CE (A) Primary School, Broadstairs

Under Heavy Fire

The truck arrived at the battlefield, the battle started. The guns were raging and bullets were flying like supersonic lightning bolts. I could see a faint shadow in the distance. It was the legendary Commander Steven. Everyone was getting their guns into position, to try and kill this legendary figure. My index finger was going backwards and forwards, trying to get a bullet to hit Commander Steven. Just then, a bomb landed in front of me. It exploded and as I took my final shot, it hit the commander. It was the end of him, Commander Steven Jones.

Lucas Harris (10)
Ramsgate Holy Trinity CE (A) Primary School, Broadstairs

When It Hit

It was a quiet day and I was practising my flying skills. My family was cheering me on as I flew like the wind. I was really tired but I couldn't stop flying now; a herd of T-rexes were still following us! It was getting late. We needed to stop but the T-rexes were still following us, then Dad collapsed. I squawked but the bloodthirsty T-rex leapt into action, tearing him to bits. That's the harsh reality of being a pterodactyl, we can't fly all day. Then I saw a giant meteorite. It hit, exploding, hitting me.

Jennifer Allan (9)
Ramsgate Holy Trinity CE (A) Primary School, Broadstairs

Something Strange

Clink! My foot hit something hard. I looked down nervously. I saw an amulet. It had many interesting patterns, like dogs, mummies and feathers. I carefully picked it up and carried on walking. I kept thinking to myself, *What could it be?* Then, all of a sudden, I saw a hole in the dusty old wall; it looked like the shape of the amulet, so I pushed the amulet into the hole carefully. *Thump!* I heard footsteps. *Thump!* I turned around and I saw a deadly looking mummy. 'Argh!'

Ella Goldwin (10)
Ramsgate Holy Trinity CE (A) Primary School, Broadstairs

Friendly Florence

There I was, lying on a smelly, dirty, hospital floor, I had so little time until I died. All I could do was listen to my own suffering pain. Then I saw a figure of a lady with a lamp, she came rushing towards me, already getting bits and bobs out. She tried to calm me down, but it was no use. She plunged something colourful and pointy into me. I suddenly felt healed. I could get up and dance. She had truly healed me. She said to me, 'I am Florence Nightingale, the nurse that changed history.'

Betsy Bridger (10)
Ramsgate Holy Trinity CE (A) Primary School, Broadstairs

Ratty Bomber

It's 1940 and I'm in a bomb crate. Suddenly, an RAF bomber pilot comes in and takes my box! Peeping through a hole, I see I'm near a bomber. By the light, it is about 10 o'clock and now I'm on board. I think if I try to escape I will get caught, so what shall I do? Do I risk it or stay put? I'm still thinking, and a door opens, so I pick up a parachute and my crate trapdoor opens. I fall out.

Timothy Allan (9)
Ramsgate Holy Trinity CE (A) Primary School, Broadstairs

Beware The Beast

The monstrosity thrust its horn towards me, attempting to pierce my soft skin. I leapt away at the last moment. I was so close I could see warriors' blood staining the white ivory. Rapidly, I got up and drew my sword. The beast rallied and, seconds later, charged once more; like a matador, I sidestepped and slashed at its guts. It let out a strangled cry, turned to me and lunged. I stumbled; the creature powered into my side. I doubled over. It spun around, leapt up and drove its horn into my flesh. No one survives the rhinotaur...

Freddie Hubert (11)
Seend Primary School, Melksham

Victorian Leopards

In the Victorian age, there was a boy called David. He was going to the Victoria zoo to see some animals. He saw some penguins and armadillos, he even saw a family of leopards. A big dad, a medium mum and a little baby leopard family. Then a leopard saw David, the dad leopard chased David around all of England, Scotland and Wales until it was really tired and fell onto the ground. The Victorian zookeeper brought the leopard back to the Victorian zoo. Then everyone was happy that the leopards were back in the Victorian zoo.

David Kryklyvyy (8)
Southcott Lower School, Leighton Buzzard

Beth Locked Up!

As I sat helplessly in the corner of the tower, a charcoal-grey rat scurried across the floor. A blackbird sat outside the barred window. Suddenly, my soot-black cat, Misty, elegantly walked in with a key and a note shoved under her collar. I crawled hopelessly towards Misty. The note read: 'Take this, bring down the queen!' So I grabbed the key, grabbed Misty and unlocked myself. I ran down the metal spiral stairs, I ran to the throne room - it was huge! There, Mary was sat, ready with a knife. Why don't I remember anything after that?

Olivia Bowditch (10)
St Andrew's CE Primary School, Sherborne

Org And John

One day, Org found John, a baby mammoth, deep in the forest and they became friends. Org started riding John in secret so nobody would know, but somehow the information got leaked and the other cavemen tried to kill John. One dark night, Org hid him in a cave to safely grow up. Once he was fully grown, Org rode John far away to another tribe who decided to make Org their chief. Not long after, the tribe trained other mammoths to obey and safely ride into many battles. They won every single one of them!

Reuben Crocker (9)

St Andrew's CE Primary School, Sherborne

The Beast

The beast was chasing me, all I could think about was an escape route! I ran and ran, the ground was shaking with every step the beast took. I looked ahead, I could see a cave, so I sprinted into it. It was dark and gloomy. I had my torch, then the cave came to an end. I couldn't move back, I couldn't move forward - the beast was blocking me. Now the beast became clearer. It was a mammoth, but no ordinary mammoth, it was the biggest mammoth I had ever seen! I screamed...

Izzy Ward (9)
St Andrew's CE Primary School, Sherborne

Fiona And Jack's Adventure

The wind blew, pebbles rumbled and trees clashed together. There it was. A big monster approached me. *Roar!* I stepped back and bit my tongue. Jack fainted. I took a deep breath.

After a couple of minutes, Jack woke up. 'What on Earth is that, Fiona?'

'I don't know but it's big!'

Jack stepped towards the big, large monster.

'Leave my sister alone.'

'Jack! Look out! It's a dinosaur! Run away! It's going to collapse!'

Makeda Powell (9)

Whitehorse Manor Junior School, Thornton Heath

The Sword

It was a quiet day in the city. The sky was calm and Arthur was strolling through the woods. He tripped over a rock and stumbled into a churchyard. Before he could touch the sword, Kay came and grabbed him. 'Get out of my way! I'm older, let me go first.' 'Why? I got here first.' Arthur pushed Kay out of the way.

'Let's see what Father says!' yelled Kay, with a mischievous look in his eyes. Suddenly, there was a strike of thunder and Merlin appeared. He told Arthur to try and pull out the sword. Arthur was victorious!

Tamar March (9)
Whitehorse Manor Junior School, Thornton Heath

Terrified Jowllyarna...

Jowllyarna was scared in the middle of nowhere. The wind was howling mysteriously, there was nobody to make friends with. Showers of rain and a big storm headed towards her. *Boom!* The lightning struck Jowllyarna. Jowllyarna fell into a deep, deep sleep.

When she woke up, days later with a bloody forehead, Jowllyarna knew there was something wrong. Out of the mist of dust, there appeared to be a gigantic reptile charging towards her. Just then, within a split-second, she ran as fast as a lightning bolt...

Ijeoma Nwaonu-Aghaluke (9)
Whitehorse Manor Junior School, Thornton Heath

We're Finished

There was a threatening storm and people were constantly getting sucked up. We thought we were toast but we had some hope. People were trying to hang on, although it was no use. Trying to stay safe, we dashed to the back of the cave. Slowly, the storm drifted away. Trouble wasn't over yet. A rhino and a sabertooth tiger came charging at us. We tried to fight it off but it didn't work. Then it ran off.

The next morning, they were back to finish us with their bloody teeth and horns. It was the end of time...

Godfrey Nkansah (9)
Whitehorse Manor Junior School, Thornton Heath

The Great Stone Age Flames

As the leafy trees waved in the swaying wind, Zig heard a boom! A big flame of heat raced down the forest and came closer to Zig's house.

Zig panicked, she couldn't believe her eyes, it was a real fire! As it came closer and closer, it began to get hotter and hotter. Zig tried to cool it down but it was impossible, it kept on spreading like it wouldn't end.

That night, Og came to see what the matter was but as he stared across the moonlit sky, he was too late - it was the end...

Hodan Ereg (9)
Whitehorse Manor Junior School, Thornton Heath

Jumble Tumbly Down The Hill

Tumbling down a hill, James bumped into a ferocious dinosaur named Ferro who was sleeping. He woke up. He huffed and puffed and he roared at James. James couldn't believe what he saw. He ran up the hill, his stomach rumbled and he tumbled down the hill again. James really wanted some lunch. Luckily, he packed a sandwich. Then Ferro ate James' sandwich. Within two minutes, the huge, strong dinosaur vanished, James looked everywhere but he was out of sight. In the blink of an eye, he was right in front of James. Then James became the lunch!

Christian Andrews (9)
Whitehorse Manor Junior School, Thornton Heath

Armageddon

The wind howled, Conker was walking on the pitch-black street. It was the Second World War. He saw bombs being dropped like a fish gliding through the sea. As he walked past wrecked houses, he saw an atomic bomb and dashed towards it. As he arrived, he saw lots of people turning in different directions. He saw the time on the clock and froze. There was only five seconds left. He zoomed like a cheetah catching an antelope. Run... Run... Run; that was all he could think of. *Boom!* He dropped onto the floor.

Omar Qamar (9)
Whitehorse Manor Junior School, Thornton Heath

The Glory Story Of Crystal Palace

Dad and I were travelling to Wembley for the FA Cup semi-final. It was Crystal Palace Vs Watford. I'd never been to Wembley before. My heart was pounding, I couldn't sleep the night before because I was so excited. We went by coach with the rest of the fans, most of them were my dad's age, it was great to see grown men cheering and singing. When we arrived, Wembley was so big, I held my dad's hand tightly so I didn't get lost. The game started, Palace had a skilful game, and they won 2-1. The glory of Palace!

Lucas Victorire-Carter (9)
Whitehorse Manor Junior School, Thornton Heath

First Hunt

There was a flash of lightning. Trees kept falling. There were two best friends. They met when they were five years old. Everything changed once they met, their mums and dads arranged a play date. They cooked food together. They played together. Then, one day, something life-changing happened, they were asked to hunt. It changed history. They got their weapons. *Slash!* But it wasn't that easy, there was another monster bigger than them... it was a T-rex! It was gathering food! Then it all went black...

Aleena Nadesan (8)
Whitehorse Manor Junior School, Thornton Heath

The King Is Born!

Arthur approached the glistening sword. He clutched it with both hands and pulled. It slid out. Arthur rushed back to Kay. Kay glanced at the sword, knowing where it had come from. He rushed to tell his dad that he had pulled the sword but his father wasn't easily fooled. He made them put it back so he could see them do it. Kay tugged and pulled with all his might but the sword wouldn't budge. Arthur then gripped the sword and it slid out again. Kay fell to the floor like he had been struck by an arrow.

Cachelle Sullivan (9)
Whitehorse Manor Junior School, Thornton Heath

Word War II Murder

I put on my cracked helmet, shot my gun. Soldiers in the German army killed some of my men. Lightning struck the ground, I was down in numbers. Running for my life, the demonic leader glared at me. The leader made flames around the field. There was a demon and an angel around me. I thought I should make peace or kill him. I wanted to show no mercy but I couldn't. Blood pouring down my neck, my gun broke to pieces. A tsunami of rain poured onto my wounds. I got shot, by Adolf Hitler. There was terror...

Emmanuel Serwornu (9)
Whitehorse Manor Junior School, Thornton Heath

World War I

The sky was black. You could hear gunshots in the distance. There were screams and shouts around my house. Once you looked outside, you could see a swarm of bullets. There were puddles of blood everywhere. There was a tick-tick-tick at my neighbour's house. *Boom!* I was terrified. I walked towards the window to see what happened. I wasn't sure what to do. There were men on the battlefield, there were hundreds of dead bodies on the floor. My roof was blown off, it was coming for me! *Boom!*

Luca Tanase (9)
Whitehorse Manor Junior School, Thornton Heath

ANCIENT ADVENTURES - THE SOUTH

The Battle Has Arrived

It was a misty, foggy day and nobody was around. Arthur and I crept towards the tent, we heard a twig break. *Crack!* We froze with fear! We were being watched; we panicked, not knowing what to do. We heard a sword slide out of its scabbard. It was time to stand our ground; we were at war. We looked all around for a weapon and saw a sword in a stone; I told Arthur he should pull it out, so he tried. It slid out like magic! Now we were really ready for battle!

Naima Maxwell (9)
Whitehorse Manor Junior School, Thornton Heath

Fire Time

The cold wind breezed past us, the ground shook and everything fell. Everyone was scared and ashes were fired at us. We got things together and ran, then I remembered I couldn't - I had to save Tam. I got Tam and ran to the lake, there were no more boats left. We were too late! We fell into a deep sleep. I woke up three or four days later, it was like I travelled back in time, it was mysterious. I pinched myself just to make sure it was not just me who travelled back in time...

Caylin Spruit (9)
Whitehorse Manor Junior School, Thornton Heath

The Chase

The wind howled in the night. I heard a noise, I was being watched. Through the darkness, I saw red, bloody eyes. I had to act quickly or I would be lunch. I smelt danger. In the blink of an eye I saw a pack of raptors, I screamed like I never had before. Their claws were as sharp as five knives combined, their teeth looked like they were enough to break bones. I went as fast as lightning but they were faster. A dead end! No escape, no choice. I blacked out...

Richard Sava (9)
Whitehorse Manor Junior School, Thornton Heath

A Dinosaur

As the dark red sun went down and raised the pale white moon, I heard a roar. I decided to follow the noise. It took an hour but I finally found the animal. I thought I saw a flash of lightning, but it was my old torch with some old batteries in it. I wanted to know what it was. *Roar!* Again, this time it sounded like a dinosaur. Was it? No, it was a beetle next to a microphone, talking into it! So I did all of that for nothing! Was it really the beetle?

Ewura Akua Asare (9)
Whitehorse Manor Junior School, Thornton Heath

Tick, Tick, Boo

I packed my heavy bags, ready to go to Egypt. When I got there, we were staring around but I spotted something - a pyramid! I told my mum and she said we could go and explore. Suddenly, it was starting to get dark. We went inside. Something howled. I started to shiver. *Bang!* The door shut. Something grabbed my leg and pulled me. I woke up in a dark place. There was blood everywhere...

Fiona Krasniqi (9)
Whitehorse Manor Junior School, Thornton Heath

Mime Time!

The lights flickered out in the mines. The mud squelched in his boots. Looking scared, Bob mined rocks until there was a shaking noise. Rocks were startled. An eye popped out. A monster! He tried to run but the monster was too fast for him. Rocks collapsed, trapping Bob and holding him hostage. He tried to get out but every time he moved a muscle, the monster growled at him...

Samuel Ponou (9)
Whitehorse Manor Junior School, Thornton Heath

Perseus And The Chimera

Long ago, in ancient Greece, there was a hero named Perseus.
One day, he was given the task to go and defeat the beast called the Chimera. It lived in a cave. When he got there he was nervous, but proud to be doing it. He looked into the cave and saw the beast. He charged towards it and kept trying to stab it but he couldn't do it. He kept trying and finally he got the beast right in his poisonous heart, and returned to town. When he got there, everyone was cheering, 'Perseus!'

Grace Glattback (8)
Whitleigh Community Primary School, Plymouth

How Fire Was Discovered

Hi, I'm a caveman and I am about to tell you how fire was discovered. It all started when I was eating raw meat in my cave. It was dark and raining, there was a big storm coming, but all of a sudden a lightning bolt hit a tree and set it on fire. I didn't know what was happening! Finally, I discovered fire and I poked it with my stick. Unfortunately, it caught on fire. I brought it back to show the others. When I got to my cave, it lit up the cave. We discovered cooking with fire!

Ryan Ryder (8)
Whitleigh Community Primary School, Plymouth

Years of YoungWriters

YOUNG WRITERS
INFORMATION

We hope you have enjoyed reading this book – and that you will continue to in the coming years.

If you're a young writer who enjoys reading and creative writing, or the parent of an enthusiastic poet or story writer, do visit our website www.youngwriters.co.uk. Here you will find free competitions, workshops and games, as well as recommended reads, a poetry glossary and our blog.

If you would like to order further copies of this book, or any of our other titles give us a call or visit **www.youngwriters.co.uk**.

'HE CAME, HE SAW, HE CONKED US'!

Young Writers
Remus House
Coltsfoot Drive
Peterborough
PE2 9BF

(01733) 890066
info@youngwriters.co.uk